The Wizard, the Farmer, and the Very Petty Princess

Daniel Fox

Cover design by J Caleb Clark (jcalebsclark@bellsouth.net)

ISBN: 1467929182
ISBN-13: 978-1467929189

FOR MY PARENTS

Ta-da!

BEFORE

There was a grim noise, an awful noise, crunching and clacking and chunking out between the graves. The residents of the boneyard, those who had fought wars, battled illnesses, been savaged by animals and capitulated to time were having their well-deserved rest disturbed by some rather impolite soul. And at this time of night those noises could warn of only one thing – trouble.

The gravedigger lurched out of his shack, ready for battle. His face usually had as much expression as one of the old gravestones around him. In his many years he'd weathered grieving families and friends, smelled the rot of decaying bodies, and none of it had earned much more than a blink. But now there was someone out there in the night playing foul with his charges, his wards, and there was a fury in his face.

He smacked his axe-handle into his open hand and called out into the fog, challenging the intruders to have the courage to face one of the living. But the digging sounds went on. The old man's voice was blanketed by the fog; the digging sounds seemed to come from all sides at once.

The gravedigger stepped and stepped again, waving his axe-handle in front of him like a blind man waves a cane. The wood clinked against the Morley gravestone (passed some fifty years ago, loving father and husband), scraped against Miller (over a hundred years gone, but will always be missed), but being too short to find the ground completely missed the open Blythe grave. The gravedigger yelped and in he went heels over head, to crash into the open casket below.

The gravedigger's curses barely made it to the top of the grave before the fog smothered them. He scrambled about in a panic, rat-like, trying desperately to not disturb the remains of the dearly departed lady. He stopped; his flailing hands had found a ring. And a necklace, complete with locket. But no body. What kind of grave-robbers went to all the trouble of digging six feet down through hard-packed earth, cracked open a coffin, and then took the body but left behind the valuables?

The noises outside his own little grave had stopped. The gravedigger stood, eyes squeezed shut, all ears, listening. Nothing. Just his own breathing, just his own heartbeat. He got to his feet, jumped, pulled himself out and up.

The fog, having concealed the enemy, finally parted and rolled and folded away, letting the moon have its way with the scene. The gravedigger's jaw dropped, he spun this way, then that, unable to lay eyes on enough at one time to convince himself that what he was seeing was true. The mysterious sounds hadn't just been a trick of the fog, they hadn't come from just one source; they had come from many sources, maybe hundreds. *Impossible!* said the gravedigger's mind. *But true!* replied his eyes.

Every grave, every crypt, every tomb had been thrown open. Ransacked and robbed. Every single one. The thousands of final resting places violated and emptied, the bodies all stolen.

The dead were gone.

CHAPTER 1

If you were to ask Idwal the farmer if this story was about him he would tell you absolutely not. He would then take you gently by the elbow and escort you from the premises and then forever after do his very best to pretend he had never met you. Stories are about singularly exciting moments in the lives of singular exciting people. Exciting moments and exciting people were the two very things that Idwal tried hardest to avoid in life.

He certainly lived in the right place. Idwal's small neat farm lay on the outskirts of what is, to this very day, considered the most boring place ever created by man. More boring than your high school math class, even more boring than church, the place was just about as exciting as watching grass grow. And not the green grass that your parents make you mow every week. Oh no, we're talking that long stuff out in the wild you barely even see because you're so excited by the trees and the ants making away with your cookies. (It's been said that there were two places in the world created by nature, instead of man, that were more boring than this town, but it's hard to verify since nobody ever bothered marking them down on a map.)

Not to give you the wrong idea. It was a neat town, to be sure. Tidy. All the buildings were kept ship-shape, fences mended and windows washed. It was just that there was no color anywhere, no zip or zing - not on the walls or the gardens or even in the clothes that the town folk wore. And the food! Eating sawdust would have been more exciting. Less nutritious, but more exciting.

Idwal made his way into town one bright sunny morning, very much not whistling a jaunty tune, doffing his cap politely this way and that to his friends and neighbors. As he strode down the main street, doing his best to ignore the cheerful sun overhead and the charming birds which sang out their greetings, he heard a peculiar flapping overhead. Looking up, he saw that a banner had been strung out over the road, stretching from one building to another. The banner was made of a number of faded brown burlap sacks that had been split open and then sewn together. Across them had been written the words PLAIN AND SENSIBLE DAY in blocky whitewash letters. Originally the words had been followed by an exclamation point, but some sensible soul had painted over the stick part of the punctuation with beige paint, leaving only the period behind.

The banner seemed to indicate some kind of celebration. Idwal looked around, not quite sure what to expect. He'd never really been a part of a celebration before, at least not in the sense you and I would think of. In this part of the world when someone's birthday rolled around you gave them a useful present, a hoe or a pair of scissors, and you made darn sure that you presented it unwrapped to avoid any sort of surprise. Weddings usually involved someone shaking your hand and then baking you something like a loaf of bread, maybe throwing some rice at you after it had been boiled to make sure it was nice and soft. Funerals went pretty much the same way.

There was quite a lot going on, at least as measured by this particular town. Almost everybody had taken the day off work. Everybody was milling around the street in their Sunday plainest. Since there wasn't much to see in terms of decoration, the good townspeople instead saw each other, and you have to admit that perhaps that isn't such a horrible thing.

There were even a couple of stalls set up along the street, although they had no particular wares to be seen. Instead one vendor called out, "Booooring! Get your drab and your blah right here!"

A second vendor, his stall unpainted and smaller than the first spoke out in a quieter voice that there was, "Nothing to see here! Nothing at all!"

A third vendor, who didn't really have a stall at all, just a board lying across two barrels, seemed to be selling, "Same ole same ole. Get it while you can, it's selling at a moderate pace." Or at least that's what Idwal thought the man was saying, he was really speaking far too quietly for Idwal to be sure.

Idwal made his way through the smatterings of town folk over to the General Store. There he waved hello to Jan, the General Store's proprietor, a gruff-faced elder if ever there was one. There were scars across Jan's face, trophies from the last of the human wars, many years ago. Jan was a focused gent, and all his considerable concentration was being put into a frightful scowl which was aimed at the banner above and all the people beneath it.

"A very fine day to you, young Master Idwal," said Jan, giving the farmer a businesslike nod. "How's the farm?"

"The same," said Idwal.

"Splendid."

"How's your Missus?"

"The same," said Jan.

"Wonderful. And the children?"

"Growing."

"Ah," said Idwal, shaking his head. "That's a shame."

"But otherwise the same."

"Oh good. So, I'm afraid the old homestead could use a lick of paint."

"What's your fancy?"

"I was thinking a robust beige with some faded grey highlights."

"Just a moment then," said Jan, heading inside, "let me check my stock." This is what passed for a joke in the town. Jan only had those two colours, it was a well known fact. Two great big pyramids made out of buckets of the stuff. The town blacksmith, Eire Tonely, had once made the mistake of enquiring about a faded pink to paint the walls of his young daughter's bedroom. Jan and the other elders had shunned him for a year.

While Idwal waited he snuck another peek along the main street. Something was different. To be more precise, some*one* was different, and new. There, in amongst all the greys and browns of the town folk was a woman, a very old woman, her brown skin weathered like an apple left in the sun. She was a baggy mess of skirts over skirts under blouses under shawls, all finished up with a pair of mismatched boots. And the colours! To say they were bright was a criminal understatement. It wasn't so much that you saw the colours of all her mismatched clothes as that the colours jumped out and poked their thumbs into your eyes. It was a drive-by rainbowing.

The crone was pacing back and forth under the banner, waving some kind of paper in the air and yelling, right *at* people mind you, that she was selling adventures. Adventures in dark forests, haunted castles, by lava-spewing volcanoes or roaring waterfalls. Adventures to face ghosts, slay ghouls, or to just generally right all sorts of wrongs. She yelled out that everyone should come get an adventure while they were hot, to step right up and take a quest that was guaranteed to change your life (said guarantee being void if a werewolf ate your face or an ogre used you to clean its ears).

A pocket of space had opened up around the old woman. She couldn't have been more avoided if she had been there trying to sell leprosy, the extra-oozy kind. And yet despite all of this, despite the noise and the colours and the sheer nonsense of what she was trying to sell, and very much despite the fact that Idwal was a respected member in good standing of this particular town, he couldn't quite bring himself to look away.

He gave a bit of a squeak and a jump as Jan thumped down the buckets of paint. As they settled Idwal's account the farmer pointed up at the banner. "What's all this then," he said. "The banner, the stalls? Why is everyone taking the day off?"

"You need to get in from your farm a bit more," replied Jan. "It's forty years of the peace don't ya know." Jan grew quiet for a moment. Idwal could see the elder travelling back to those times, to the wars. There was old remembered violence running in Jan's veins, ghosts of lost friends haunting his heart. Jan sighed and looked out at the people of his town. "If we have to celebrate, I suppose the peace is a good reason. Still," Idwal watched Jan deliberately pull the scowl back onto his face, "celebrating peace with a load of ruckus and tomfoolery... It's completely without sense, I tell you."

"Quite right," said Idwal.

"Could be worse," said Jan. "Imagine the nonsense going on elsewhere."

"Indeed." Idwal nodded his head in the just-so manner the elders used when they were disapproving of something, an occasion which occurred more often than not. "It's the noisy ones that cause all the trouble."

Having proved himself agreeably disapproving, Idwal picked up his two buckets of paint and started up the road toward his home. However he got only a few steps along before the door of the town's only inn, the Pale Pony, was opened, and from it stepped the young maiden of Idwal's heart's desire, Gretal. She was quite a pretty young woman, despite her efforts to the contrary. Her white-blonde hair was pulled back into a bun so severe that it looked like a form of punishment. Her clothes were neat, tidy, but unflattering to what very well have been a fine womanly figure underneath. Or perhaps the figure wasn't all that fine. Nobody really knew. Gretal was, in Idwal's earnest opinion, the very epitome of the deliberately dull town.

She greeted him with a smile and they began to walk together. "You haven't been to the fair?" she said.

"Oh no, not me," said Idwal. He hefted the buckets of paint. "Just scampered in for a bit of business, that's all. It's straight back to the farm for me."

"Good," said Gretal, and she favoured him with another smile.

"I've just had a thought," said Idwal, and it was true, this idea really had just come to him in the moment. "It occurs to me that you and I get along rather well."

"That's true," said Gretal.

"Well-" said Idwal, but then a brochure was thrust into his face by a grimy brown hand. He turned and found the colourful old woman standing next to him, bouncing up and down on the balls of her feet.

"Adventure, young sir?" she said in her rough crow's voice.

Gretal pushed the brochure out of the way. "Certainly not," she said, and took Idwal by the arm to lead him away. "You were saying?"

"Right, well," Idwal cleared his throat. "We've known each other since we were children, so it's highly unlikely that there's anything about us that we could surprise the other with. You have your inn, I have my farm, and that's just the way we'd like things to continue on. I think it's fair to say that we're both of moderate ambitions and cautious accomplishments."

"True."

"So I can't help but wonder-" Another brochure shot up in front of Idwal's face.

"If not an adventure," said the old woman, "how about a quest?"

"No," said Idwal, gently pushing the old woman's hand aside. "Thanks awfully though." He turned to Gretal. "Where was I?"

"Cautious accomplishments."

"Right. Well. So those are all the reasons why I think we should probably get married. What do you think?"

It didn't take Gretal very long to decide. She stopped walking and stared at the sky, weighing the pros and cons. She chewed on her lower lip a moment more, then shrugged and gave Idwal another smile. "I don't see why not." And that was that.

This proposal was, by the way, to be ever after considered the third-most romantic occurrence to ever take place in the town. Second place was generally acknowledged as the time, some ten years back, when Branwen Farley had been out for a walk and had come across the farmer Tadwell trapped under a cow he had been milking. There was no real malice in the cow, it just seemed that after all that teat-yanking she'd needed a bit of a breather, so down she went. Branwen had been unable to get said cow to budge be it by honey or by vinegar, so she had made the trip back home to fetch her older brother Stil who was respected as being somewhat of an authority in the bovine species. Stil had returned with Branwen to the farm, sized up the situation, slipped on a glove, and plunged his arm into the cow's behind right up to his shoulder. To say that the cow moved would be an understatement. The farmer Tadwell was saved.

If this story had originated in any other place, you could rightfully expect to hear that Tadwell and Branwen had made some sort of romantic connection - gazing into each other's eyes, sighing at the very thought of the other's wonderfulness, that sort of thing. But not so in this town; here, that was as far as the tale went. Tadwell and Branwen never actually connected after that; still, it *had* been nice of Branwen to make all that effort.

The top-most romantic story of the town revolved around how Stil Farley managed to retrieve his glove from the cow's rear end.

Idwal and Gretal, having given the nod to the whole marriage idea, leaned their heads together to plan the event out. There was much talk of not having decorations or too fancy a cake, how twigs were under-rated as floral arrangements, how they would have beautiful babies but not too beautiful, ha ha.

"A daring deed maybe?" The old woman was at them again, a new note of desperation in her voice. "Look!" she said before either of the young couple could cut her off. She shuffled out her pack of brochures. "I've got a good one here. Let's you cut the head right off of a virgin-eating dragon."

"A virgin-eating dragon?" Gretal sniffed. "You mean out there?" She waved a dismissive hand around, indicating the world at large. "Poor creature must have gone and starved to death by now. Ta-ta." She grabbed Idwal's arm again and marched him away.

But as Gretal went on planning their bland upcoming affair Idwal couldn't help looking back over his shoulder. The old woman stood all alone in the middle of the road, all slumped and sad. A body couldn't help but feel a little bit sorry for her. Was it more outlandish to talk to the old woman, or to make believe she didn't exist? Talking to people was an every day thing; the idea that the old woman wasn't there was absurd. And absurdity was an enemy of normality. So...

Idwal gently detached himself from Gretal. He gave an embarrassed nod to each and every one of her objections even as he made his way back to the crone.

"Any sales?"

"Not a one," sad the old woman sadly. "I just can't understand it. Look at my brochures here! I made them all by hand! Drew every dragon scale, laboured by candlelight to fill all these foreign landscapes with enchantment and wonder. I even enlarged all the heaving bosoms." She flipped up one particular brochure that promised the damsel you rescued to be extremely grateful. Said bosoms were indeed of the heaving variety. Idwal was suspicious; a woman able to stand upright with such endowments seemed more mythical than the manticore than was rearing over her.

"Yes I see," said Idwal. "It's just that in all of the great human kingdoms you've chosen the very worst place to try to sell such wares. We don't much go in for the daring-do around here. In fact we try to avoid stepping in just regular old do as much as possible."

"Piffle!" cried the old woman. "Everyone needs at least one good to-do."

"Not us. We prefer the quiet and the calm."

"How do you know?"

"I'm sorry?"

"How do you know? How do you know you prefer one thing when you've never known the other? Can't be done, can it?"

"I just know."

"Double-piffle!" The old woman started to shuffle through her papers again but stopped as a baker trooped by, a basket of fresh bread perched on his shoulder. The old woman's stomach was just as loud as the rest of her. People down the street could have held a conversation with its growling.

"Have you eaten?" said Idwal. "Do you have a place to sleep?"

"I'm afraid it's no to both."

"Well..." Idwal looked back down the road. Gretal was standing next to Jan, the both of them watching him. Watching? Judging, more like. Even though he knew that he was now definitely stepping into the realm of the abnormal, the most seriously not-every-day, he took the old woman by the arm and led her down the road. "Come along then," he said. "We'll fix you up and get you on your way to somewhere more profitable first thing in the morning."

"You're very kind. You're sure I can't interest you in the tiniest of crusades?"

"I'm sure."

"A trek?"

"No thank you."

"A sally-forth?"

Back at the General Store Gretal winced as Idwal shouted a final *NO!* at the old woman and threw his hands up into the air.

"Ach," said Jan, spitting on the ground. "It's always the noisy ones."

And that was how Idwal met the old woman.

CHAPTER 2

If you were to ask Princess Willuna of the Family Owl if this story was about her she would tell you that of course it was, and think you rather simple for having to ask such a silly question. She'd admit that not all stories were strictly about princesses, sometimes they were about knights or kings and the like, but a beautiful princess pretty much guaranteed that your story would be that much better. The fact that she was really quite beautiful (not bragging of course, beautiful princesses never bragged about how devastating their loveliness was) elevated Willuna to the lead role.

There was one man she wouldn't mind sharing top billing with. The good King Anisim. The King of the Family Wolf. A great warrior. A great king. Young and handsome and utterly incapable of doing any wrong.

Willuna very much intended to marry him. Anisim, young though he was, was considered by most to be the greatest king in all the human kingdoms; being married to him would ensure that Willuna was the greatest queen. Which meant that she would be adored even more than she already was. The more loving and admiration Willuna received, the happier it made her. After all, what were princesses but living receptacles for praise?

There was however one pesky detail that had escaped Willuna's attention - she wasn't a very lovable person. She was certainly beautiful on the outside; but that beauty, as they say, only went skin deep. She was vain and petty. It's not that she was a bad person in and of herself; she just didn't know any better. Being her father's only child, and looking so very much like her passed mother, her father had sheltered Willuna from the harsher and more cruel qualities of the world, which in some cases meant sheltering her from the truth. He had spared the rod and spoiled the child.

Word had come that Anisim had already arrived, a day early for the great feast. Willuna was sure that could mean only one thing; Anisim was here to ask her to marry him. Why else would he rush to her side? They would announce the engagement at the feast and everyone would be completely happy for them. The women would envy her, but Willuna was determined to be gracious and kind to those less fortunate than herself... which was pretty much everyone.

As Willuna sat combing out her long hair, thinking up compliments she could pay to all the other women who weren't blessed enough to be in her shoes, her two handmaidens Ilsa and Elsa were creating a hurricane of fabrics as they tore through Willuna's collection of dresses.

"This one!" cried Ilsa, preening in front of a mirror, holding a dress of pale rose up before her.

"No, *this* one," said Elsa, shoving her sister aside.

"You have no taste."

"You have no hips."

This had been going on for some time. Willuna had quite the number of dresses and gowns. There were mountains of chiffons on the chairs, rolling hills of lace draped across the four-poster bed. Almost all of it was pink.

"What do you think, your Highness?" said Ilsa.

"Hmmm?"

"Which dress do you think?"

"For the feast," said Elsa.

"All those dreamy princes," sighed Ilsa.

"With their princely shoulders."

"And princely arms."

"And royal behinds."

The girls giggled as only girls can do. Willuna smiled and lay down her hairbrush. She joined the girls by the mirror and held up the dress that Ilsa handed her. "There's only one set of arms and shoulders and... whatnot for me," she said, "and it is kingly."

The girls sighed. "Anisim," said Ilsa.

"He really is a cut above," said Elsa.

Willuna shook her head and tossed the dress aside. "I've known since we were children that we were meant to be together." Willuna moved to a large wide cabinet that stood in a special place of honour along the wall. It was made of rich dark wood, the surface heavily decorated with carved flowers of all sorts. The whole of it was waxed and polished so heavily that it seemed to be emitting its own light instead of merely reflecting what came from the candles around the room. Willuna grabbed hold of the two biggest carved roses of the cabinet and pulled open the doors, letting them swing wide.

Inside the special cabinet was a very special dress. Willuna's bridal gown. Have you ever seen pictures of old weddings; images of princesses and ladies marrying their dukes and lords? Have you seen how lovely the young women looked, knowing that quite possibly the whole world would be taking at least a peek, if not a good hard look, at the way they were dressed? Take your favourite bride in your favourite dress and hold her in your mind. And be ready for disappointment. Compared to this dress your choice of bride looked frumpy.

It was the only bit of clothing that Willuna owned that wasn't pink. It was a clean gleaming white, the white made to seem all that much more pure as it hung there against the dark wood of the cabinet. It had slim laced shoulders leading to a neckline that was polite and demure, as befitting a bride who would come to her husband unblemished, as it were. The waist was slim, but loose - Willuna knew from experience that any feast, especially a wedding feast, thrown by her father was bound to have mountains of food, so she'd deliberately had the dressmakers leave room for belly expansion. The waist flared down into overlapping skirts that had been fashioned to look like the petals of a newly opened rose. It was a stunning thing, this dress. Quite literally. Every time the three young ladies laid eyes on it anew they stopped in their tracks, caught up in its beauty.

Willuna pulled the dress down from out of the cabinet. "I've even been practicing," she said.

"Practicing, m'lady?" said Elsa.

"That's right!" Willuna handed one sleeve off to each girl, then went down on one knee before it. "You are the very greatest princess in the whole of the human kingdoms," she said in a gruff imitation of a man's voice. "You are the most beautiful and gracious, and you will look wonderful on my arm. You would do me the greatest honour if you would consent to be my bride, Queen of the Wolf Kingdom."

A curtsey from the dress, twisted this way and that by the handmaidens, just so. Willuna stood, and together the three girls danced the dress around the room. "Anisim is the greatest king in all the lands, and so I shall be the greatest queen. I will be beautiful and proper and perfect. Our people will be happy and cheer us as we go by."

There was a knock at the door. Ilsa went to answer it as Elsa and Willuna carefully rearranged the wedding dress back in its place of honour. There was a thump and a bang and they turned to see Ilsa with her back pressed against the door. Her face looked like it was having a battle with itself, teetering from fright to joy and back again. There was no way to tell which expression was winning.

"He... he..." panted Ilsa.

"What's going on?" said Willuna.

"Did you get stung by a bee?" said Elsa. She turned to Ilsa. "She's a bit allergic. Her breathing gets a bit wheezy like this and her face gets all puffy. Well, puffier."

Ilsa was shaking her head no and no and no! She pointed a trembling finger back over her shoulder, indicating the hallway outside the door. "He's here. Anisim. King Anisim, I mean. He's coming to see you right now!"

Panic! The girls dove into the dresses, shoving them under the bed, under the mattress, into the cupboards, quick quick quick!

And then it came. A knock at the door. *The* knock at the door. The knock that signalled the greatest moment of the girls' lives. (Willuna most of all of course, but Ilsa and Elsa were quite invested as well. They had been like sisters with the princess ever since they were wee little things. One time, when Willuna was six and the twins four, Willuna had tripped and scraped her knee. Willuna had just brushed herself off and ordered the offending rock executed - which basically involved her father ordering his honour guard to drop the stone into the castle's moat. On the other hand Ilsa hadn't stopped crying for a week. When Willuna was eight a very young magician, barely into his teens, had come to the court to show off his tricks. Willuna had been the loudest to laugh when an astonishing variety of animals had escaped from the boy magician's sleeve before their appointed time. It hadn't helped any that the young princess had been responsible for the mass escape - she'd snuck up behind the boy and released all of his animals. Ilsa and Elsa had made sure to point and laugh just as loud as the princess. All of which is to say that their lives were as intertwined as creepers of ivy. Willuna's joy was the twins' joy, and of course the same can be said for their shared sorrows.)

Willuna dropped herself into a chair positioned just so, so that the light coming through the window behind her would shine through her thick, rich hair. Elsa stood in attendance at Willuna's right hand. Willuna took a deep breath, hoping to settle her galloping heart, then gave Ilsa a nod. The handmaiden gulped and swung open the door.

Anisim, King of the Family Wolf, strode in. Ladies, and gentlemen of the persuasion, have you ever encountered a man so handsome that he made the back of your knees sweaty? A man so ruggedly good-looking that you had to fan yourself after he left? Anisim looked like the brother of that man, the brother who got all the looks. His shoulders were broad and moved with muscle under his black shirt. His chin was square and strong, and his teeth perfect in an age when dental care basically involved avoiding hitting yourself in the mouth with a rock. He was still wearing his travelling clothes, his black cloak with its silver lining stained from the roads, his boots had been more or less scraped clean but it had been a hasty job and bits of dried mud still clung here and there. Willuna felt her heart pick up its already quick pace; Anisim was so madly in love with her he hadn't even bothered to clean up before he came to give her his proposal!

The king came over to Willuna and took up her hand to kiss it. "Willuna," he said, "look at you, you're a vision."

"Thank you, your Highness, you look fairly well yourself. You may go girls."

The twins didn't move. The both of them stood, identically, with their jaws open, eyes teary, hands clasped tightly in front of them.

"Girls?" Still nothing. Willuna gave Anisim a smile then reached over and pinched Elsa's hand. The handmaiden jumped then ran over to drag her sister out into the hall. They gave one final peek back into the room at this moment of moments, then shut the door behind them.

"Wine?" said Willuna.

"Please."

Willuna stood and went to a sideboard to pour them both a goblet. She arched a pretty eyebrow at the king. "No chaperone?" she said. "What will people think?"

"This sort of thing is best done in private."

That was it. That was the clincher. Not that Willuna had ever had a doubt that Anisim was going to do the right thing and propose to her, but still, now it was completely for sure. What else would a brave man like this prefer to do in private? Well, besides, you know, *that*. Willuna dipped her head, hoping Anisim couldn't see her blush. She raised her goblet, ordering her hand not to shake. "Shall we drink to our future?" she said.

"About that." Anisim drained his cup, then moved past the princess to fill his cup again. "I wanted to do this properly, I owe you that much."

Willuna heard the words, but they came through muddy and mushed, like her head was underwater. She was really quite worried that she would faint before Anisim got the words out. She wondered if he would take the thud of her body hitting the floor as a great big yes.

The king turned to her, looked down into her eyes. "We've been friends for a long time."

"We have."

"And we always will be."

"We will." Looking up at him like this, so close, she noticed dark circles around his eyes. He looked quite tired. He must have ridden night and day to get here. Maybe he had been worried about all the princes that were arriving for the feast, worried one of them might snatch her up first. None of them had a chance with her of course, still, it was good for Anisim to know that he couldn't just take her for granted. He'd have to earn her love, each and every day. The princess imagined there were a lot of presents in her future.

The king rubbed a weary hand along that magnificent jawline. "My father was a very serious man," he said, "and he ran our kingdom in a very serious manner."

Willuna nodded. "It's a very serious business."

"I'm glad you see that. It's a world of nothing but sacrifice. As far as... marriage goes I'll need the support of a serious woman."

"Oh," said Willuna, "absolutely." Willuna reached up and took his hand in hers. Felt the callouses, the manly roughness of the skin. Her heart kicked into a charging gallop as Anisim smiled. Here came the question! *The* question! This was it!

The Wolf King said, "I'm glad you're taking this so well."

Willuna cried back, "Of course I..." Willuna stopped, took a moment to replay back in her mind what Anisim had just said. He was glad she was taking this so well? What kind of proposal was that? "Um, just a moment," said the princess. "What? What am I taking?"

"There's plenty of boys downstairs-"

It hit her. Right in the gut. In the head, in the heart worst of all. She felt like she had tripped and fallen flat on her belly, all her breath had been knocked out of her. Anisim wasn't proposing. The exact opposite in fact, he was taking away any chance that he would ever propose. Willuna shook her head. "Why?" she said. "Why are you doing this? Is it me? Is there something wrong with me? That can't be, I know there's nothing wrong with *me*, I'm perfect. What's wrong with *you*?"

"Whenever my father was down on me you were my refuge," said the king. "You were my place of light and laughter. But now things are growing dark. There are all these reports of ghouls and ghosts and who knows what else slipping through the night. I have to protect my people, Willuna, I have to be serious. And that means I can't let you distract me."

"Distract you?"

"Well, you have to admit that you're... surprisingly strong." Anisim yanked his hand away and gave it a shake.

Willuna's senses just weren't coming through as clear as they should, everything was going through her mind too slow, like wading in neck-deep waters. What *did* make it through wasn't making any sense - she was the perfect princess. People just didn't go around not proposing to her. "I'm a distraction?" she said.

"My father's footsteps lead into a world of chain and mail. You, you're chiffon and lace."

"But I thought you loved me! You have to love me! I'm beautiful and charming and... and..."

"I do love you Willuna. For what you are. I want you to be able to stay that way. Tell your father that I'm sorry I wasn't able to stay for the feast." The king went over to the door and opened it. He turned back and said, "I said it before and I'll say it again, I do love you. But I can't marry you. People expect me to be their sword. I can't have them thinking you took away my edge." Out he went, closing the door behind him.

That is how Princess Willuna of the Family Owl found out that she was not a serious woman.

CHAPTER 3

Idwal woke, stretched, thought evil things about the crinks that had taken up residence in his neck and back. He yawned, feeling like he had hardly slept at all. Last night was a half-remembered eon of half-wakefulness, of being just barely submerged beneath the tideline of sleep and being unable to go all the way under. His skin was clammy, his mouth sour.

Rubbing his face, he looked down at the bench he'd slept on, considered giving it a kick. He looked around, stupid with fatigue… why had he slept on the bench again? He spotted his bedroom door, closed. Of course. He'd let that old woman have his bed. He'd probably be the subject of village gossip for some time to come. Maybe he could get the crone out and away this morning before too many people were out to see her leave his house.

He gave a quiet knock on the door. "Old woman?" he said. There was no answer. He tried again, louder. Again, nothing. He turned the door knob, peeked inside. Then opened the door fully. No old woman to be seen. The bed was made, it looked fresh, like it hadn't been slept in. But after feeding the old woman last night he had escorted her in, showed her where there were spare blankets, left her a candle, and bid her good-night, closing the door behind him. But she'd gone and slipped away in the middle of the night. Idwal looked around for a clue - maybe a note. Nothing. It was like the old woman had not been in the room at all.

Idwal had his breakfast - eggs, bacon, toast, slices of tomatoes pulled fresh from his fields. After washing the dishes and putting them back in their appointed places he stepped out his back door, lighting his pipe, gazed with love across his neat orderly fields. Except this particular morning there was a lump, a very large lump, being all lumpy right out in amongst the vegetables. Being a very organized type of fellow, Idwal was sure he hadn't sown any lump-seeds, so the sudden appearance of just such a lump in his fields was a highly unexpected occurrence. He went out to see just what variety of lump he now suddenly had on his hands.

An hour later everyone of any importance from the village had gathered around in a circle, careful not to tramp the vegetables, and was peering down at the mystery object. There was a multitude of head-scratching, and a smattering of poking with sticks by the elders. Idwal stood outside the circle of people, wringing the end of his shirt around his knuckles. He'd assured everyone that he had never planted such a thing, not in *his* fields, no sir, and that he had absolutely no idea how it had got there.

Gretal stood off to the other side of the circle of people, dabbing her moist eyes with a handkerchief. She was quite upset. She had, just yesterday, agreed to the marriage proposal of a properly normal young man. And now today she had found out he was the kind of person who had strange lumps in his field. *Unusual* lumps. She was still fond of Idwal, but she wasn't at all sure that she wanted to be the wife of a purveyor of unusual lumps.

"Please Gretal, all of you," said Idwal, "you must know that I didn't do this on purpose."

"It serves you right," said Gretal, wringing her handkerchief, "messing about with strange women."

All of the village's eyes turned to Idwal. Strange women?

Idwal waved his hands. "No no no," he said, "it's okay. She was very old."

Which didn't help things a bit. All those eyes narrowed. Idwal realized he had managed to go from lump-grower to sexual deviant in the space of four words. It was most desperately time to change the subject. "So who's going to help me get rid of it?" he said.

Jan, of the General Store, ran a finger along one of his many scars. This was a sure sign he was concentrating. "I don't know if that's the wisest course."

"What?" said Idwal. "You can't possibly think I should keep it!"

"No," said Jan. "But I also don't think one should just go off willy-nilly and destroy something so obviously," Jan coughed, not liking to say the word, "magical."

The villagers gasped and took a collective step back from Idwal.

"What can I do?" said Idwal.

"You must take it to the king."

"Me?"

"You."

Idwal jabbed a finger out, pointing at everywhere but here. Safe here, normal here, the only here he knew. "Out there?"

"The king is an extraordinary man used to dealing in extraordinary things." Jan jerked a thumb back over his shoulder at that miserable field lump. "And if ever I laid eyes on the extraordinary..." Jan took pity on the miserable farmer, threw a comforting arm around the young man's shoulder and guided him a few steps away from the others. "I know you've never been outside the village before, and I have to admit I kind of envied you for it. But the truth be told, this may turn out to be a good thing for you."

"I'm not so sure," said Idwal. He looked back past Jan at Gretal standing there, being consoled by the villagers. Poor girl. Imagine getting engaged to someone and the very next day finding out he's involved in doing strange things with weird old women.

"You're a young man. You've got a young man's blood running through your veins. And one major ingredient of such blood is fire. A burning to see, to smell, to touch and taste the new and the unexplored. Hold your tongue boy, I know it to be true. I was once a young man myself. Besides, it would be unnatural for you not to feel that way. So! You go out yonder. You see, you touch, you taste. You take your specimen there and give it to the king. And then you come home and appreciate what you have here all the more. Otherwise, you'll forever be known as the farmer who forced the village to find some way to deal with his magical field lump."

Idwal's mind whirred and clicked and came up with absolutely no counter-argument. "All right," he said, "I'll go." He walked over to Gretal. "Right after we're married."

Gretal eyes went wide. "Me?" She flapped her handkerchief at the atrocity. "Marry that?"

Idwal slumped. Turned to Jan. "Which way to the king?"

That is how Idwal discovered that inviting strange women into your bed can result in your having mysterious lumps.

***

Imagine you're a farmer of a very limited worldy experience, and you're setting out to cart this darned heavy horribly magical lumpish thing off not to the dump or maybe into the presence of the local magistrate, but to the king of all people. Bloody hell, right? And as you're getting ready to step out of the village, which has been your whole world up until now, your feet are dangling because the magical thing is too heavy for your two-wheeled hand cart, so some of your town folk start stuffing rocks into your back-pack while they're giving you helpful advice like keep your nose clean, have a safe trip, and try not to change too much, and you're weighed down enough so that your feet can touch the ground, you'd think the woman you're scheduled to marry would have a kind word for you, wouldn't you? But no, she's still all weepy and somehow blaming you for this whole ordeal, like being kind to a hungry old woman is a monumental crime, and the best she can give you is that she "hopes" that she will marry you when you get back and your life returns to sweet blessed normality, well... chances are you'd be a bit grumpy.

Idwal certainly was. He mumbled out of his village. Grumbled along the king's high road for hours, and didn't come out of his funk until he noticed that the people he was sharing the road with were all annoyingly happy. Oh yes, he thought, you enjoy your gallop you dirty so-and-so's. Like to give *you* a couple of magical lumps. Lots of angry little thoughts like that passed through his head as lone travellers turned into couples, and those into small groups and those into what might fairly be described as small caravans. All of them happy, all heading his way, all travelling into the city that surrounded the Castle Owl.

One moment Idwal was pulling his cart along the well beaten dirt roads of the country, the next he was on stone. The rumbling of his wooden wheels changed their tone. He rounded a final bend in the road and then there it was, the city. Idwal's foul mood was completely squashed by awe. It was gigantic, stretching across his view from side to side. A tall wall of white stone stood immediately before him, a large gate open across the road to admit the many visitors. Beyond the wall the city sloped up the gentle rise of a hill, going up and up and up until it met the walls of the castle itself.

The Castle Owl. It too was made of clean white stone, now turning a reddish-orange as the sun sank into the west. The flags of the royal family, a white owl on a background of red, flew from every tower's point. The castle had popped up in many a story that Idwal had heard in his youth (not that a great many fantastic stories were told in his village - usually parents would tuck their children into bed by telling them how one operated a plow, or perhaps a gentle rendition of how one should rotate one's crops). Idwal had never seen even a drawing of a castle before; but somehow this particular example nonetheless seemed to snap exactly into what Idwal had expected in his mind, like he somehow had an unfinished puzzle at home and managed to find the final missing piece a great distance away. The castle was, in Idwal's mind, exactly as a castle should be.

He was holding up traffic. People behind him gave him good natured grumbles, encouraged him onward and upward. He shut up his gaping jaw, grabbed up his squeaking cart, and walked himself into his first ever city.

There was disorder, and chaos, and cacophony, and the whole of it seemed utterly and ridiculously happy. The stables and shops and pubs and inns that were normally part of the city had sprouted stalls, proper stalls (unlike the hackneyed affairs in his village), selling just about everything imaginable.

Here! Get your hands on a divining rod that could sniff out not only fresh water but also your neighbour's secret stores of wine and ale. *There!* Buy yourself a dream catcher that actually caught dreams in its web and kept them there so you could read them like pages of a book the next morning. It boggled Idwal's mind that everyone was so casual about nestling clearly magical items right up against the everyday and the ordinary. Such a thing would never have been allowed back home.

Keeping the castle's spires in his sights Idwal slowly wound his way upwards through the city, his head turning this way and that, trying to take in everything at once. He spotted a stall with a bright painted sign proclaiming this a kissing booth. The proprietor was a cheerfully pretty young lass, her hair pulled back in piggytails. Leaning over the counter of her stall in her exceptionally low-cut peasant's blouse she gave Idwal a quite vivid reminder of the damsel in distress from the brochures of the old woman. The kissing girl gave Idwal a great big smile and beckoned him over with a waving finger. Idwal blushed, fumbled to raise his cap, made apologies, mumbled about being engaged, and stumbled himself right back into a man the size of a bear.

Idwal turned and looked up up up. The bear man frowned and looked down down down. A smile broke through the bear man's wild beard. Quite a sweet smile really, unexpected on such a dangerous looking fellow. Idwal breathed a sigh of relief. Until he realized that maybe the wild man was just happy to have someone to pound into jelly.

"Oho!" said the wild man in a voice that rumbled like not-so-distant thunder. "Another one!" The wild man flipped a coin through the air. Idwal followed the coin with his eyes and saw it land in the hand of a man standing under a small banner that had "Archery Contest!" painted in a handsome flowing script. The admirers around the bear man parted and Idwal saw an open lane. At the far end were hay bales with archery targets pinned to them.

"Oh no," said Idwal, "I don't think you want me, I've never-"

"Come on lads," rumbled and grumbled the wild man, "can't have the lad thinking ill of Owltown hospitality."

One of the wild man's group tossed another coin to the contest's purveyor. Lickety-split the wild man picked up a bow as long as Idwal's body, fitted an arrow, pulled back the string, his arm cording with muscle, and let fly. The arrow zinged its way down the lane and cut through the target half a hand-span from the bull's eye. The crowd let out a great cheer.

Accepting his due praise, the big fellow thrust the bow and a fresh arrow into Idwal's hands. Idwal looked at the unfamiliar objects in his hands. He'd never been hunting. Still, how hard could it be? There was a little notch in the end of the arrow, the string must go in there. So, put arrow on string, pull string back, aim at the colourful circles on the targets, and let go. Easy.

Only it turned out, not so easy. Notching the arrow went easy enough, but pulling the string back required a ridiculous amount of strength. The burly man beside him had managed to pull the string so far back that the bow had nearly bent in half. Idwal could barely get the string to move. But with all those eyes on him he wasn't just going to give up. So he strained a little harder, pulled the string a tiny bit back further, concentrated on the target, the tip of his tongue stuck out between his teeth. He let fly! Sort of. The arrow tumbled out over the fist holding the bow and went down pointy-end first into the ground by Idwal's foot. And then it flopped over.

There was a bit of silence from the crowd. Idwal wondered if he was blushing hard enough for people to actually hear it. But then the wild man broke out into a booming laugh and gave Idwal a friendly slap on the back so hard it nearly made his eyeballs pop out.

"Ho!" he boomed. "Ho ho ho! Didn't want to show me up in front of my hometown ladies eh? There's a man for you! There's a sport! I think we'll have to give him a suitable show of thanks." The giant looked around his crowd of friends and admirers. "What shall it be?"

A voice cried out from the crowd, "Becky!"

And then the whole of the crowd agreed, "BECKY!"

A new lane parted through the crowd. Right back to that tempting morsel in the kissing booth.

"Oh," said Idwal. "Oh no no, oh I couldn't-"

Idwal tried to make for his cart but the crowd picked him up and passed him overhead, happy hands trading him along until Becky was able to lunge up, grab him by the ears, and plant a great big kiss right on his lips. Laughing, the crowd put the farmer back on his feet, and with a few final friendly claps on the back they went on their way. Idwal gave Becky the kissing booth girl a woozy smile, tipped his cap, and made his wobbly way back to his cart. Of all the magical things in all of the magical stalls Idwal had seen in this magical city, Idwal was willing to give the buxom Becky top billing.

It took Idwal a moment to remember what he was doing in this strange place. But then he grabbed up the handles of the cart and continued on his journey up the hill to the castle. Becky waved bye-bye.

That's how Idwal learned that it's not always such a bad thing to come in second.

And also that he was a terrible shot. Just absolutely horrible.

***

It took another hour for Idwal to make it all the way up to the gates of the castle. There had been diversions every step of the way. The castle itself was a blizzard of people, cleaning, carrying, calling out names of lords and ladies. A happy blizzard, smiles everywhere. Despite the crowds that should have overwhelmed him, Idwal was surprised to find that he smiled right back. He passed more contests, wishing he had just a little bit of talent with the throwing axe, or log-rolling, or the rapid eating of pies. He passed musicians and crowds of dancers, wishing that he had some experience with the drum or lute. He even passed an additional kissing booth or two, wishing that he could stop blushing so hard.

It was a surprisingly good time, when all was said and done, except for one peculiar moment. Just as he was making his way up the final few feet to the castle's walls a large dark carriage, pulled by four large dark horses, rumbled by and through the gates. There were no symbols or signs or livery or crests painted on the cart, not that Idwal would have recognized them if there had been. It was strange, but the black cart dampened Idwal's happiness for just that moment, like that one cloud that chills the breeze on an otherwise warm spring day. Then the cart was gone, passed through the gates, and the chill was gone.

Finally arriving at the gates Idwal informed a guard of his business there that day. The guard could scarcely bring himself to believe the farmer until he had a peek at the thing in Idwal's cart, hidden under the tarp.

"Well that's a sight," said the guard. "If not for my own eyes... It's not dangerous, is it?"

"I don't think so," said Idwal. "Unless of course it rolls on top of you."

"And it's a present for the king, eh? Well, that's alright then, the king likes presents. Follow me."

So Idwal followed. Across the drawbridge which spanned a wide water-filled moat. Under the raised portcullis with its nasty downward points. Through a gate in an inner wall, across what was probably referred to as a courtyard, and into the castle proper. Idwal followed the guard, hauling his squeaky cart, through the kitchens where a thousand and one things roasted and bubbled and baked and broiled. They passed through a storage room where ale kegs, big as houses, were lined up one after another in a row as long as the main street of Idwal's village.

After this hallway and that turn they arrived in an area decidedly less workman-like and more suited to royalty. There were no workers at all here, only two guards, much more splendidly dressed than the guard who had brought Idwal this far, standing before two gigantic wood doors crossed with gold bands.

"Right," said Idwal's guard. "I sent a boy ahead so they'd know you were coming."

"Well that was very nice of you," said Idwal.

"Wasn't it? So you wait here, listen for your name, my friends here with the lovely shining armour will whisk open the doors, and in you go to present your present to the king. Easy as falling off of the old log. I'll leave you to it."

"Right," said Idwal. "Well thank you very much for all your help."

"Think nothing of it," said the guard, waving good-bye over his shoulder.

It wasn't until the guard rounded the corner out of sight that Idwal began to panic. "I'm sorry," he called out, "did you say I'm supposed to present it to the king? Me? But-"

Idwal heard from the other side of the doors, "Idwal the Farmer with a present for His Majesty, King Torquil!" boomed out in the voice of someone who very obviously made their living booming things out. The two guards swung open the doors.

Idwal the farmer, from the most boring man-made place on the planet, found himself looking in the faces of every king and queen of all the human kingdoms.

"Uh," said Idwal.

An awful silence followed. Idwal thought he could actually hear the beads of sweat trickling down his back.

"Go on," whispered the guard to his right.

"You can do it lad," said the one to his left.

Idwal forced his right foot forward, them commanded the left foot to catch up. One step, two step, and so on. He made his way down the clear central aisle, his cart wheels squeaking in an embarrassingly loud fashion with every revolution - why hadn't he gotten that fixed? On either side of him were stout wood tables. At every table sat a royal family, their house banners hanging over them from the rafters overhead. Idwal supposed he must be walking by kings and queens, lords and ladies and knights famous enough to have songs sung about them in their own lifetimes. He couldn't quite bring himself to look, his eyes kept dropping down to the floor right in front of him.

After an agonizingly long walk he finally made it to the raised bit at the end of the hall. The dais, he supposed they called it. Funny word that, dais. The day is what, exactly? And why would you want to sit on it?

He nearly jumped out of his skin when a young woman's voice said, "Daddy, you have to talk to Anisim before-"

And a man, presumably the daddy in question, replied, "Now's not the time love."

Idwal peeked upwards. Realized he still had his cap on. Whipped it off. A long table stood crosswise on the dais before him. Behind it sat Idwal's own king, the King of the Family Owl, Torquil. Much to Idwal's surprise, the king was a bit of a roly-poly man, he didn't quite match the image Idwal had made in his head when he heard what few stories passed around his village. In those, King Torquil had been a beast of the battlefields, a ferocious and unstoppable warrior. The man seated before Idwal, behind the platter of devoured turkey legs, looked like your favourite, and slightly naughty, uncle.

Beside the king sat a lovely young woman dressed all in pink. Idwal's guess was that this was the Princess Willuna. She didn't look all that happy to be there. She was pouting, and maybe it was just the smoke in the room, but Idwal thought she might have been crying. She didn't seem to have touched any of the food on the golden plate in front of her.

The king looked down at the boy from the country with an eager look on his face. To Idwal's surprise the king's legs swung back and forth in the air, he was too short to reach the ground from when seated. "So!" said the king, all vim and vigour, "I hear you have a gift for me."

"Yes," croaked Idwal. He cleared his throat and tried again. "Yes your Majesty. I found it, well, it was... see there was this woman... um... The village elders figured that it being of a somewhat important nature it should go to our most important man. So..." Idwal flapped his hands in a gesture that might have been taken for a voila! or a ta-da! or maybe just an attempt to get rid of mosquitoes. "...here."

"Oh!" cried the king, "I just can't wait any longer!" He dropped to his feet, grabbed a sword from a nearby guard, and rushed in a surprisingly nimble fashion to Idwal's cart. With three quick and sure swings the ropes were cut. The king whipped away the tarp. The mystery object stood revealed.

Utter silence in the great hall.

King Torquil stepped around the object, eyes wide, arms wide, measuring. "Willuna," he said in awed tones, "do you see?"

Willuna thumped her head back against the back of her chair. She rolled her eyes. "It's a turnip daddy."

"But what a turnip!" And indeed it was. There's no need for us to go into other great turnips of times past, none of the rest ever came close. This was a turnip for the ages. Imagine the biggest fruit or vegetable you've ever seen at a fair. This turnip would kick sand in its face and then take its girl.

There was no applause. There was a bit of muttering, and a single dry cough. Nobody quite knew if it was proper etiquette to applaud enormous vegetables, no matter how fine a sample of the species they might be. Everyone looked to Torquil for his reaction. After all he was their host and this was his gift.

The king spun around to Idwal. "This may very well be the most amazing thing I've ever laid eyes on, and you're talking to a gentleman who's been drinking with dwarves." He bellowed out to the stewards lined up at attention against the walls around the room. "Bring this fellow a chair!" He turned back to Idwal. "I absolutely insist you join us tonight and tell us all about your fabulous turnip techniques." He grabbed Idwal's hand and pumped it like a thirsty man pumps for water. "Thank you," he said, "thank you thank you thank you!"

The room erupted into applause. Except the princess who just shot the farmer a dirty glare. The king steered Idwal up onto the dais and had the stewards place the chair right next to him. The rest of the assembled royals went back to stuffing their faces.

The king grabbed up a gold plate, tossed the turkey bones to the floor, and plunked it down on front of Idwal. He threw on any bit of food he could grab - turkey legs, roasted potatoes and vegetables, slices of ham - a small mountain of food that piled up as high as Idwal's chest. It was more than the farmer usually ate in four or five days.

"Daddy," said Willuna on the other side of the king, "I want to go."

"But you haven't touched your food," said the king. "Just a bite or two, that's my pretty little petunia." Torquil leaned back to Idwal. "I'll bet it was the soil."

Idwal was busy shoving aside an eruption of gravy to see what kind of meat was underneath. "I suppose so, your Majesty."

"The water, perhaps?"

"It might have been."

The king waved a good-natured finger at Idwal. "You're keeping secrets from your king."

"Honestly your Highness, never! I'm telling the truth!"

"Relax my boy, I was kidding with you."

"I didn't do a single thing different, your Grace. I actually try my very hardest to avoid 'different'. The only thing that's really changed in my life is that the maiden of my dreams agreed to marry me."

"Oho! Congratulations!"

"Thank you your Majesty. Oh, and there was that old woman. Anyway-"

The king frowned. "Old woman? What did she look like? She didn't happen to be wearing-" A porter leaned in and whispered in the king's ear. "Ah, yes, right right..." He waved the porter away. The king patted Idwal's shoulder. "To be continued. Duty calls. But first!" The king fished around in his long sleeves (which had apparently been used more than the fine linen napkins) and came out with a small leather sack which he pressed into Idwal's hand.

Idwal opened the sack to find it full of gold coins. "Oh no, your Majesty, I couldn't. The turnip was a gift."

"Then consider it a wedding present." The king stood, a trifle unsteady, and raised his goblet. His voice cut through the merriment, bringing all eyes to himself. "Kings and Queens! Princes and Princesses! Dukes and Barons and all other such, a toast! When I was Willuna's age the thought of peace would have had no place in what passes for my mind. I was far too busy dreaming about which of your bottoms I wanted to paddle next!"

A large man, bigger even than the wild man from the archery contest, stood up under the banner of the Family Bear. "Ha!" he said, "I'd like to see you try!"

Idwal tensed. Was this how wars were started? Luckily, the rest of the room laughed. Idwal couldn't say he understood royal humour, but right then he was very glad that it existed.

"No no," King Torquil waved the Bear King down, "happily those days are behind us. I'd much rather attack some more of those roast chickens. At any rate, my friends, I say this with all the joy in the world, to the peace!"

Goblets were raised, voices replied, "To the peace!"

King Torquil cleaned out his cup, then turned back to his guests. "And now in keeping with this happy theme of unity I would like to present to all of you fine boys my daughter, Princess of the Family Owl, Willuna. Isn't she lovely? Isn't she just lovely?"

Applause applause.

The king peered out at the assembled tables, searching out princes. "Now let's see if I can remember the names of all you fine boys."

"No need daddy." Willuna stood and made her way around the table, stepping down off the dais. She circled around the tables. "I know everyone here and exactly what they have to offer." She stopped behind a particularly fat prince and tapped him on the head. "Round as a tub," she said. She moved to another table, pointed at another prince who was astonishingly tall and fantastically skinny. "Good for dusting."

Up at the head table King Torquil was starting to sweat. "Ah, my dear..."

She tapped yet another. "And here's one who is twice the voice at half the size. What fun!" said Willuna. "How exciting! My heart is all aflutter. Who to choose? Who to marry?" She flopped down into her seat and slumped. She flapped a hand at the guests. "You go ahead and pick one for me daddy. I await your decision with bated breath."

There was a tense quiet. A bad quiet. It hung in the air and Idwal thought maybe a war might break out after all. Forty years of peace wiped out by one peevish girl. On the upside, Idwal figured that if he made it out of this room alive he'd be able to get free drinks from the story for the rest of his life. His calm, quiet life, that involved no royalty whatsoever.

"Ah, yes, well..." said King Torquil, casting about for some way to ease the tension. "Entertainment!" He clapped his hands. "Send in the magician!"

The great double doors at the far end of the hall were thrown open. And then the torches winked out.

This is how Idwal learned that war is always only ever about a half-dozen insults away.

CHAPTER 4

If you were to ask Bodolomous the magician if this story was about him he would say no, but it *should* be. He was, after all, a man who had ventured where even goblins fear to tread in order to study, to learn, to grow greater than any witch or wizard that had ever lived before. Here he was in a great hall stuffed full of nobles and knights who already had people singing songs about them years before they were due to die off, but could any of them snuff out all of the braziers and torches in the room with a single gesture? Not bloody likely.

There weren't any shrieks or cries from the assembled royals, they were by and large all veterans from the wars and had nerves tempered like steel. Bodolomous did hear, on the other hand, a lot of knives being snatched up from trenchers and plates. He found himself taking a surprised step back, sincerely hoping that he wouldn't get stabbed before he got to the good bits of his show. After all, this evening had been a long time coming for him.

"My lords and ladies," he called out, and thrust out his arms. Assembled around him, crouching and bobbing, were a dozen wiry people dressed in jester outfits, their faces painted like clowns. They sprinted outward, fanning around the room. "I give you my most humble thanks for this grand opportunity to perform my poor tricks."

The jesters, never making a sound, tumbled around the room in the most amazing display of acrobatics that had ever been seen by human eyes. Goblins had once seen a grander display, put on by fairy folk, but no one is really sure that counts since the goblins were busy setting the fairies on fire at the time. The jesters cartwheeled, somersaulted, vaulted and leapt, springing their way over the long tables until they were spread all around the room.

As one, the jesters threw streamers across the room, the thin fabrics unspooling in the air. At a word from the magician the streamers began to glow like they had fires within them, filling the room with just about every colour imaginable. Bodolomous took in the sight of the greatest names in the human kingdoms, their faces upturned and coloured by his magic streaming lights, their eyes full of childish wonder. He was sure he could have gone around the room and picked all of their pockets at that moment, and not a one of them would have noticed.

He let his eyes move to the high host table. There sat the King Torquil and, where was she… ah yes, the princess. Much to the wizard's satisfaction her face was also upturned, her eyes watching as the glowing streamers slowly began to drift down out of the air.

Bodolomous raised his hands, ready to wow the room with his next bit of magic. But just then his eyes happened to flick to the other side of King Torquil and found the oddest thing - a commoner. And *so* common. *Ridiculously* common. His clothes were so plain that it was like he had taken a look at all the other common people in the world and had decided to dress down from their example. Bodolomous had the knowledge of the ages in his head, and he had had to beg and borrow and plot and steal to gain permission (which was an affront in itself, really - these silly people who happened to be accidentally born into their stations should have to gain permission to watch him perform) to put on this show. How did that plain boring bugger rate sitting next to the king? The world was a cruel and unusual place.

He put the plain fellow out of his mind for the moment. He hadn't come this far to screw up things now. He turned his eyes back to the princess once more to remind himself why he was here. And then he smiled his showman's smile and said to the royals, "Wonders never cease."

This was how Bodolomous the wizard learned that he had competition.

***

The wizard found the princess wandering the castle's parapets alone. Her personal guard stood some ways off, having been told to give her some space. It was a simple task for Bodolomous to slip past the guard and into the princess' presence.

She spun around, hearing his footsteps, and was delightfully surprised to find him just an arm's length away. "How did you-"

They heard the grinding of feet on stone as the guard turned, first thinking that the princess was addressing him. Seeing Bodolomous, he started forward, angry at himself for having allowed someone to sneak past.

The wizard had studied the princess for quite some time. Not up close, because that would probably have gotten his head chopped off. His surveillance had at first been accomplished from afar, through stories and rumours. The same two truths always seemed to come through - that the princess was beautiful, and that she was a vain little creature. Bodolomous was able to better confirm this later, as the years went by and his powers grew, from a much more personal perspective. He was sure that he knew how to handle her; he knew just what to say. Or at least he very much hoped he did; that lumbering guard was quite large and mean-looking. "Forgive me your Grace," he said with a low bow, "I didn't mean to frighten you."

The princess responded just as Bodolomous hoped. She stuck her nose in the air. "*You*?" she said. "Frighten *me*?" The very idea of it was beneath her. She waved off the guard. Bodolomous ducked his chin so that the princess couldn't see his smile. Not all tricks require wizardry.

Bodolomous peered over the castle's wall. Below them the city spread out down the hill. People below celebrated - making fireflies of themselves with sparklers, making themselves hyenas with their laughter, some of them making themselves pregnant with regrettably ugly people and a great deal of ale. The wizard sniffed. He had been one of them, once. "Noisy," he said, his voice all disdain.

"They're happy," said Willuna. Then she stomped her foot. It wasn't an especially impressive stomp seeing as how her foot was tiny and in a little pink slipper with a little pink bow on top. It reminded the wizard of some kind of overly sweet pastry. The princess pouted. "It's not fair."

"So," said the wizard, getting down to business. "Did you enjoy my show?"

We have to be clear here, this was the crux not only of this conversation, but of the wizard's entire life. Everything he did and was, since he had been a very young man, was focused in on this particular question, asked of this particular princess. In his travels he had gone to very dark places, horrible places were just the flora had given him nightmares, never mind the fauna.

He'd apprenticed with fiends, and been mentored by some of the most rotten souls on the planet. (This isn't to say that all the people who used magic were evil, it's just that the ones who would be considered "good" and "just" were always so picky about what sorts of people they passed their knowledge on to. At the beginning Bodolomous probably would have passed through all their soul-searching tests, but he was starving for knowledge, and quite frankly just didn't want to spend all that extra time polishing up his spirit to a squeaky shine. And once he'd started working with some of those nastier sorts he figured none of the more heroic types would have wanted anything to do with him.)

He'd left bits of himself behind, in all those dark places and with all those dark people. Bits of his soul. Some of the shinier bits, the types of bits that he supposed the most noble of heroes had in spades. Sometimes he missed those bits of himself, and he got to wondering what he would have made of his life if he'd left a few more of them intact.

But those were other paths, *this* path led to this particular princess and this particular question. So, you can understand that Bodolomous was somewhat put out when the princess replied, "Hm? Oh, the show. The magic, right. I'm afraid my mind was somewhere else."

Her mind was somewhere else.

Her mind was somewhere *else*?

Where else could it have been? There were the streamer lights and flames that shaped themselves into dragons and sea shells that roared like lions and shadow puppets that picked up goblets and drank them dry. There had been the inhuman tumbling of the jesters, the dark stories that had been played out by knives and forks and chicken bones come to life. Twenty years of fear and terror and loneliness and sweat and blood had poured out of Bodolomous. He had given a show that had astounded royalty. He had put on a performance that was even now being woven into songs.

And the princess' mind had been somewhere else? That was not the answer Bodolomous had worked for all those years.

Rage came flooding into him. Dark and angry thoughts that many of his mentors had tried to bring to the front of his being through the years. Bodolomous had fought back against those tides, he knew that if he'd committed deeds as evil as those of some of his teachers he'd never be allowed into the presence of the princess.

But right now, chucking the girl over the parapet seemed a fantastic idea. He even took a shaking step toward her, but realized that guard was still somewhere behind him. As much as he desired to do something just tremendously awful to the young woman right then, he had no desire to end up with a pike stuck into his back as a reward.

He clasped his shaking hands together and grit his teeth. He'd been silent for a little too long and the princess had turned to look at him. He gave her what he hoped passed for a smile as he raced for something, *anything* to talk about. "Might..." he said, and stopped to clear his throat. He tried again. "Might I enquire as to the name of that fellow seated up next to your father, the one dressed in the dreadfully humble attire?" It wasn't really a subject that was going to calm the wizard, but maybe at least he could direct his rage elsewhere instead of it present focus of the princess' long slim neck that would fit oh so nicely in his hands.

"Who?" said the princess. "Oh, him. He's just some turnip farmer." The princess turned away again.

Good thing. She missed seeing Bodolomous' face grow a fantastic shade of raging red. The veins stood out in his neck, another started throbbing its way down his forehead. Bodolomous believed he now knew what cursed people felt like. First the princess missed his life's work, and now he finds out that some rube from the country got to have dinner with the king? "Gah-" he sort of said, and sort of just choked out. "A turnip-"

"I know!" said the princess, spinning around.

"I journey for years upon years to learn my dark arts..."

"Here I am with my world crashing down around my ears..."

"...all with the faintest hopes of being in your presence again..."

"...and all daddy wants to talk about is fertilizer!"

"...and all this time I could have just invested in some dirt and a hoe?"

"Stupid farmer!"

"The miserable peasant!"

"Well," said Willuna, "I won't stand for it!"

"This cannot be allowed to stand!" said the wizard.

"I won't just be cast aside!"

"I'll show you all!"

"He wants a serious girl, I'll show him serious!"

"If not fame, then infamy!"

Willuna pushed up her sleeves. "Look out world," she said, "here I come!"

"Prepare yourselves," cried Bodolomous, waving his fist at the sky, "for I bring doom!"

And then there was quiet from the parapet, just the two of them standing there in their dramatic poses, panting. They looked at each other out of the corner of their eyes.

"Did you say something?" said Willuna.

"Nope," said Bodolomous.

And off they went, both on their separate way.

And that was how two sad and overly proud people completely avoided learning anything and inadvertently set in motion events that would threaten everything and everyone they'd ever known.

CHAPTER 5

The dawn came on thick and muggy. So did the people of the town. Hangovers were the main topic of conversation, and all of those conversations were in whispers. A couple of the braver roosters inside the town's expanse tried to greet the morning, but gave up after boots were repeatedly thrown at their heads.

Idwal snored away. He was usually up with the first light of dawn, but he'd been kept up very late the previous night, and had been stuffed full of an incredible amount of food. Staggering away from the feast in some small hour of the morning, he'd been escorted by a steward to a guest room in one of the castle's towers. The room was round, the stone walls hung with tapestries showing knights on horseback fighting off all sorts of scary creatures. Instead of scaring him the scenes made Idwal somewhat content, he felt safe knowing there were people trained in the business of bashing goblins in the faces with oversized hammers, chopping off the heads of giant snakes, that sort of thing. The tapestries weren't defined enough to show expressions on the faces of the knights. He wondered if they were scared, or bellowing out some battle charge, or maybe just businesslike as they went through a mental list of all the steps required to slay a dragon. Poke with sword, check; block fire with shield, check; hack off great big head from great big neck with great big sword, check and check again!

A finger reached out to almost poke Idwal's shoulder. But then it shrunk back. The finger was royal, and not used to touching dirty commoners. The finger withdrew, and was replaced a moment later with a fire poker. The poker jabbed at Idwal's shoulder, gently, then with more force.

Idwal jerked awake to find the princess Willuna standing over him. "Your Highness?" Idwal tried to bow, though it didn't come off all that well as he was laying on his side. Not that the bows he did while standing up were something to write home about, but at least they didn't make him look like he had a tummy ache. It was after this mockery of a bow that Idwal realized the situation they were in. "You're in my room," he said. And then his eyes went wide and he pulled the blankets up around his chin. "I'm not dressed!"

Willuna rolled her eyes. "A dream come true for me as well. Clean the great quantities of wax from your ears and listen closely. The man I love, the one I actually find myself attracted to, he's interested in marrying a particular kind of girl."

"Ah," said Idwal, relaxing a bit, "and that's not you?"

"But it will be." Willuna put her hands behind her back and paced around the room. "I need a mentor," she said, "someone who can teach me to be serious."

"Well, it's true I'm not particularly well known for my jokes but-"

"You?" Willuna snorted. "You're funny. No. What I want is for you to help me sneak out and choose the right person for the job."

"Sneak?" said Idwal. "There's sneaking?"

"Do you really think my father is just going to let me openly wander off with some stranger? Of course he isn't. So I must be quick and quiet."

"Your father is really very fond of you. If he catches us-"

"Don't worry," said Willuna, "I have a disguise." The princess pulled the scarf from around her neck and wrapped it around her hair. She then proceeded to tuck in her chin and walk around the room with an astonishingly dramatic limp. "Hey," she said in what Idwal supposed was supposed to be a man's voice, "who is that old woman?" Willuna answered herself in a high falsetto. "Not the princess Willuna, that's for sure." She stopped and smiled at the farmer. "You see? Even *my* beauty can be disguised, if you know what you're doing. So? What do you think?"

"Your father is going to be so angry."

Willuna glared. She really didn't know what to do with insults, she'd never heard one before. "He's certainly a very passionate man," she said. "Once he shows an interest in something he can worry at it for years. Did I mention he's taken quite a liking to you?"

Idwal smiled. "Really? Me?"

"Absolutely you. You and your silly gift. He's infatuated with the thing. He's sure to try to pry your dirty farmer secrets from your dirty farmer mind. But being such a busy man, he might have to do said prying in dribs and drabs. It could possibly take months."

"Months?"

"Maybe even years. Didn't I hear you say you had some girl back home waiting for you? Maybe you're lucky, maybe you have the kind of girl who would wait her entire life for you," she eyed Idwal up and down, "though I can't imagine why. On the other hand, an entire lifetime is a very long time to wait. Especially if you're waiting on someone who is less than perfect. Are you perfect, farmer?"

Idwal was silent, thinking thinking thinking. He'd always tried to be the best citizen he could be, according to the dictates of his home town. But he'd never been quite right, had he? Despite his best efforts, there were always going to be the whispers and rumours that he had adventuring in his blood. And the giant turnip hadn't made things any better. No, in

Gretal's eyes he was probably not perfect. All of a sudden he felt a clock ticking away in his head - how long until Gretal gave up on him?

He knew the princess could read the answer in his face. She smiled at him. "You have fields that need farming and a girl that needs marrying. Get me my mentor and I'll make sure my father is distracted long enough for you to make your getaway."

"You're sure this is what you want?" said Idwal, worrying the edge of the blankets with his hands.

"Aren't you?" said the princess.

***

So down to Owltown they went. Idwal sweated the whole way down, doing his best to give the guards a pleasant nod and tip of the hat. Behind him, shuffling ever so slowly, was the princess in her ridiculous disguise. All the while Idwal trembled, his mind tripping from one corporal punishment to the next should they be caught. Would it be the noose? The executioner's axe? Maybe he would be drawn and quartered. Idwal wasn't exactly sure what that entailed; having your portrait sketched didn't sound so bad, but that "quartered" part sounded awful.

Finally they made it to the marketplace, the princess dragging her supposedly bad foot behind her. Idwal asked one more time if the princess really wanted to go through with this.

"Wouldn't it be easier to go back to your life?" he asked.

"No," said the princess in a hushed voice, "it would not. My normal life involves me not being married to the greatest king in all the lands, and me not being the greatest queen. Who in their right mind would want to be normal?"

"I would," said Idwal, "there's nothing I want more."

"Normal is boring. How can you ever win anything by doing the same thing day in and day out?"

"Maybe one doesn't win anything extra, but one doesn't lose what one already has. Your Highness."

Willuna flapped a disgusted hand at him "On with it," she said. "What do your peasant instincts tell you?"

Idwal looked around. The market was packed with all the extra people who had come to the town for the celebrations. The stalls and stores were doing a brisk business. Everyone was smiling at everyone else, which made it difficult to figure out if anyone was of a serious nature. Finally Idwal directed the princess' attention to a woman with thick auburn hair who was giving a coin to a beggar. Idwal pointed and said, "What about her?"

Willuna peered over at the woman. "She just gave that man money."

"Yes, that's right."

"But what did he give her in return?"

Idwal shrugged. "Satisfaction?"

"That's it?"

"What more does one need?"

"You can't be serious. That woman is unwise and has nothing to teach me."

Idwal looked around again. He spotted a gentleman with a walrus moustache paying a baker for a loaf of bread. "Will he do?

Willuna watched the man for a moment. "I didn't see him bargain. He didn't even give the tiniest of debates."

"I guess not."

"Then how does he know he didn't pay too much?"

"Maybe he knows the baker. Maybe he knows already that it's very good bread."

"He is cowardly and afraid to fight for what he wants. And you, farmer, are beginning to grow tiresome."

Idwal was beginning to wonder if there was any sort of punishment for giving a princess, especially a spoiled, vain princess, a good talking to. It might be worth suffering through a thumbscrew or two to give her a piece of his mind.

But instead he forced a smile and looked around a third time. A high screeching voice erupted from the next row of stalls over. It was a terrible voice to listen to, all whiny and doing a fairly good impression of a couple of crows fighting over some scraps.

"Blackguard!" yelled the voice. "Criminal! Miscreant!"

The princess forgot her limp and squeezed herself between two stalls to hurry over and see what all the fuss was about. Idwal was content to let her go, but figured his punishment might be worse if instead of just escorting the princess out of the castle without a guard he actually went ahead and lost her, as pleasant as the thought might be. In that case they might skip right over the pleasant drawing part and go straight to the quartering. He sucked in his belly and squeezed through the stalls after her.

He found her watching an older man, his skin-and-bones body dressed in black, waving a bony fist at a fish merchant. His face was beet red, the colour travelling over the top of his bald head and down the back of his neck. "You see!" he screeched at the crowd that was forming around them. "Take heed!" He thrust an accusing finger at the merchant. "This crook spies an old face and takes it for an easy mark! Beware the fish monger! Beware!"

Idwal watched as Willuna took a step forward and addressed the spindly old gent. "Tried to overcharge you, did he?"

The old fellow grasped the young woman's hands, locking on to the one person in the crowd who wasn't treating this like a spectator sport. There was something about the way the old man looked at the princess, a hungry possessive sort of look, that just didn't sit right with Idwal. He stepped up beside the princess, trying to get her attention. "Maybe we should move on."

Willuna didn't look at him. "Maybe you just want to go spend your reward."

At the mention of the word "reward" the elderly gent's greedy look shifted to Idwal, sizing him up. Idwal liked the looks of the man even less now.

"So," said Willuna, forgetting about the farmer, "you fought back, did you?"

"I did," said the miser. "Tooth and nail, my girl, tooth and nail."

"And you're sure you were overcharged?"

"To a criminal degree!"

"Oh come now," started the fishmonger, but Willuna waved him off. She might have been in disguise, such as it was, but there was still a presence about her, one that expected her commands to be obeyed, and it was a strong enough force to quiet the merchant. "You're perfect," said the princess, returning her eyes to the old man.

"Him?" said Idwal. "*Him?*"

"I'll be married by this time next week," said Willuna, her eyes never leaving her new prize. "Rejoice, farmer," she said, "you're free to go. Enjoy normality, I know I won't." With that, she took the miser by the arm and led him away, turning a corner out of Idwal's sight.

There was a moment when Idwal weighed going back to one of the guards and telling them that the princess was walking off with some strange man. But there was that ever-looming chance that he might be held responsible. And the princess was getting what she most wanted, or so she said. Most of all, Idwal just desperately wanted to get back to his life.

No, it was home for him. Idwal returned to the castle, picked up the bag of coins the king had given him, reclaimed his cart from the great hall, and began the walk home.

CHAPTER 6

Willuna was escorted to the Miser's house. It sat alone, not so far from the city. It was a craggly old thing, the paint peeling from the walls, the walls themselves bowed and sinking at odd angles into the ground. The windows were completely covered over with grime and soot. The walkway up to the door was a bunch of old round slices of log and stones, none of which had been properly sunk into the earth, but just thrown on the ground making a rough wavering path from the roadway to the door.

The house's insides were no better. Litter and garbage lay on every surface, coated with dust. Old rank unwashed clothing hung from the backs of chairs. The air itself was old and used up. Once inside, the Miser plunked down an astonishingly large laundry basket with a broken handle.

Willuna edged cautiously toward it. She could smell the soiled clothing in it before she actually saw anything.

"So," said the Miser. "You're here to learn eh? To become serious. Well, here lies your first lesson of the day." The Miser pulled a sock from the pile of clothing. It was so stiff with grime that he was able to tap it against the side of the basket.

Willuna's stomach started turning queasy rolls. "What will this teach me?"

The Miser considered the sock in his hand. "Courage," he said.

The Miser told her to hop to it, and dashed out the door on some very important business.

And so Willuna did the Miser's laundry, wondering all the while if Anisim was thinking of her.

That night she slept in the laundry basket, a rough blanket pulled up to her chin.

The next morning the Miser kicked the side of the basket until Willuna was awake. He fed her a breakfast of toast crumbs and egg grease, and then hustled her outside. He plunked down a leaky wooden bucket and a wash-rag at her feet.

"What's this for?" Willuna said, trying to stretch out the kinks in her neck.

"The windows," said the Miser. "To help you see more clearly. This is the pathway to wisdom." The Miser insisted she hop to it, and then left again to do more of his miserly business.

And so Willuna washed the Miser's windows, the grime so think that it was like the glass had curtains clinging to them. And while she scrubbed, up and down, back and forth, her hands going red from the water and soap, she wondered how much more Anisim would appreciate her if he could see how much effort she was putting into learning to be serious.

That night Willuna slept in the basket again, but in the middle of the night the Miser took away her blanket, because he was feeling a chill.

The third morning the Miser returned with the bucket, this time throwing in a scrub brush that was missing many of its bristles. Willuna stared at the bucket for a moment, her tired mind having trouble thinking of words.

"The floors," said the Miser, "so you'll learn to poke into every corner. This is the way to build up an enquiring mind." And away went the Miser once again, to do whatever it is that Misers did.

Willuna looked down at the floors in despair. A cockroach scuttled by, completely ignoring her, leaving a little trail in the dust. She wondered if this was how common people went about their common lives, feeling sad and weary all the time. Or did common people enjoy this? Did common women look forward to a new broom the way that Willuna anticipated her new weekly dress? She supposed that once she was queen she could work out some way to reduce the drudgery of the common person, but what if that meant taking away their source of happiness?

She pushed that queen stuff out of her mind and kneeled down to get to work. As she scrubbed away she thought of Anisim and how much he better bloody well appreciate her doing all this work just to make herself more attractive to him.

The fourth morning found Willuna in a better mood. Even though she had barely slept at all in her basket, she was up and awake before the Miser. She waited impatiently for the old man to groan his way out of his bed, and then confronted him in his office. As she entered the Miser hid a small bag from her eyes. If Willuna had cared about such things she might have recognized it as the bag her father had given to that farmer the night of the great feast. But she wasn't interested in bags that morning, her only concern was conducting her business as quickly as possible.

"Eh? What do you want?" said the Miser, not liking his coin counting to be interrupted. He wrapped his arms around the small bag and peered up with suspicious eyes at the princess.

"I have hung your laundry and washed your windows and scrubbed your floors. Your horrible, horrible floors."

"So?"

"I would like my wages please."

"But there is so much more I can teach you!" wailed the Miser. "There's the walls that need painting and furniture that needs mending and I won't lie to you, I could use a good foot rub." The Miser propped a foot up on his desk. One of the very ugliest toes ever known to mankind stuck up through a hole in his sock. It was dirty and yellow and shaped like the type of potato you would instantly discard as being inedible.

Willuna shivered. "I've had lessons enough, thank you very much."

"Fine." The Miser turned his back and fished around in the coin sack. "Right then," he said, "three coins for three chores."

"I would take nothing less," Willuna sniffed.

The Miser handed over the three coins. Willuna had to tug them free from his fingers. "Are you sure you won't stay longer?" said the Miser. "You're ridiculously che- Er, efficient. You're surpassingly efficient."

"I'm sure," she said. "As of today I have acquired courage, wisdom, and an enquiring mind. Plus three coins. And now I'm off to claim my husband. Good day."

With that Willuna stuck her nose in the air and walked out.

And that's how Willuna learned that self-improvement was really rather easy. (Her belief that she had no desire to be a commoner was also strongly confirmed.)

***

Across the human kingdoms, beyond bogs and swamps, up a sharp mountain and down a narrow crag, there was a great dark castle. A proper castle. Not some squared-off thing with shameful white in its walls, but a castle of spires pointed like spears and walls with crumbling parapets that looked like some giant's rotting teeth. A castle to make you believe in evil.

Across the molding drawbridge, down around spiralling stairways and behind secret panels, in the very bottom of the castle dug far into the ground where no sunlight had ever touched, Bodolomous kept his laboratory.

The stone room flickered with torch-light. The walls were dank and darkly moist, the dim corners filled with cobwebs.

Across wooden tables cauldrons bubbled and beakers coughed up noxious green smells.

Worst of all, one end of the long room was filled with bodies. Some were far gone, nothing left of them but skeletons and wisps of clothes. Others were fresh, looking more asleep than dead. They were piled with no reverence for the departed souls; fish in a market were laid out with greater care.

Bodolomous sifted through the bodies, looking for an arm. He pinched at one, strong but too bulky. He groped another, thin but too weak. Finally he found an arm just right, strong with a working-man's muscle but not so bulky as to get in its own way. He cut away the sleeve from the arm, then cut away the arm from the body. He took the arm to one of his tables where a body had been assembled from the finest legs and the best of torsos. Sewing the arm to the empty socket, he muttered words far too foul to be repeated here (and to be honest, the words were spectacularly hard to spell). He dabbed some potion, waved a particular wand, and just like that the body jerked, and jerked again, and then the eyes popped open. A new jester was born.

"Up you get," said Bodolomous. The jester sprang up to its feet, then to its hands, and then vaulted off the table, spinning in the air to land on its feet. "Rotter!"

Rotter, the one particular jester that Bodolomous had bothered to name, came scampering up to fawn at his cloak's hem. There wasn't really anything special about Rotter, but Bodolomous had wanted to be able to talk to somebody by name, and so one day he'd pointed at one and told it that from now on it was called Rotter. Bodolomous had sewn bells onto the points of Rotter's jester cap. Previously the wizard had kept losing him in the crowds of jesters, now Bodolomous just had to follow the little tinkling sounds.

"Right," said the wizard, "make sure this new fellow gets all dressed up nice. I won't have any minions of mine tumbling about with their goodies just flopping this way and that. People would think I'm not good enough at being evil to afford to properly clothe you. Off with him."

More jesters came and led their new sibling over to a pile of scrap clothing off near the bodies. Bodolomous grabbed Rotter's arm to hold him back. "Not bad eh, all this?" He waved a hand proudly at his beakers and bottles and potions. "Looks pretty evil to me. I mean, honestly, if you were some innocent little school girl who got dragged down into here, this would frighten you, right?"

Rotter nodded his head and pretended to quiver.

"Ha!" said Bodolomous, "exactly right! Miss my show, will she? Well, not this next one, I guarantee you that. This will be a display that they'll never stop talking about. Folks will be all like, 'You 'eard about Bodolomous the wizard?' 'Oh, don't say his name just out loud like that. He's the Most Evil Man Alive, you know.' 'I did know that, as a matter of fact. Everyone knows that. He's just that famous, Bodolomous is. Anyway, you 'eard about what he did to the Family Owl, how he sent in all his min...' What?

Rotter was shaking his head. The jester scurried over and tapped the glass of one of the many large mirrors that hung on the walls around the room. He scurried back, took Bodolomous by the sleeve, and drew him over to the mirror.

Bodlomous closed his eyes, concentrated, and muttered a few choice putrid syllables. The glass in mirror twisted, the reflected image of the wizard sinking away. Like air bubbles tumbling up from under water, the glass of the mirror filled with an image from far away. Bodolomous was looking into a bedroom of a castle, a castle made from white walls. There really wasn't much to see. The room was filled with a lot of pink things - blankets, cushions, the upholstery on the chairs, and not much else of interest.

"Well?" said Bodolomous to his minion. "What am I supposed to be looking at?"

Rotter waved his hand, encouraging the wizard to keep looking.

Bodolomous turned back to the mirror and passed his hand before it. The image changed. It was another room in the Castle Owl, one that was much less pink. "I'm still not seeing anything."

Rotter tapped a long claw-like nail on the mirror, pointing at the bed of the room.

"So?" said the wizard, "there's nobody there."

Rotter gave his head a vigorous nod. Bodolomous waved the mirror back to the first image, that room that was hopelessly pink. Nobody in that bed either. He changed the image to a third room, and a fourth. Every bed and every room was empty. "Where is everyone?" he said. "Is this thing working?" He gave the mirror a couple of good stiff slaps on its side. Nothing changed.

He rushed the mirror from one bedroom to the next and the next, finding no one. "Someone should be in bed by now," he said. "Nobody respectable should be up at this late hour." He turned to Rotter. "That's why I'm still up." Rotter nodded. "Why didn't you tell me about... about..." Bodolomous pointed at the mirror and the bedrooms beyond. "...this?"

Rotter opened his mouth and pointed inside.

Bodolomous threw up his hands. "Oh here we go about the tongue again. I've told you and I've told you, they rot away too quickly. And the alternatives..."

One time Bodolomous had tried to appease Rotter and his empty mouth. It was true, tongues just went bad too fast to be transplanted with any success. So the wizard had tried other parts. He'd really rather liked the baby arm sprouting out of the jester's mouth, it looked properly obscene, but every surface got incredibly sticky whenever the jester tried to enjoy an ice cream cone.

"How could they do this to me?" said Bodolomous. "Here I am working day and night to build myself an army and there's nobody for me to frighten. Just completely rude if you ask me. You," he said, pointing at Rotter, "grab up some of your chums and bring me word of what's going on over there in the Owl Kingdom. I won't have somebody mucking up my bid for infamy. Off with you now."

Rotter scurried away, joined by one jester, then another, and yet another.

"Go!" shouted the wizard after them, "go and find me someone to scare!"

That was how the dark wizard Bodolomous found out that someone out there was interfering with his plans.

***

Willuna's heart nearly stopped when the feet hit her in the face. Her mind had been kingdoms away, with Anisim, imagining their greatness together. Feet dangling in the air were quite the shock.

She picked herself up off the ground, dusting off the offensive dirt that had the nerve to cling to her dress. She looked up and found the farmer up in the air, a rope tied tight around his waist, pinning his arms to his sides.

"You!"

"Princess!"

The farmer tried to make her a bow, but did it poorly. The princess had to admit though, it probably wasn't the easiest thing to do while dangling in the air.

"You ought to watch where you place your feet."

"I will try my lady. Terribly sorry my lady."

"Look at you. You can't even hang yourself right. Why are you even here? Why aren't you back home farming your farm and wifeing your wife?"

"Ah, well, yes, I was on my way, you see. But your miserly friend caught up to me-"

Willuna held up a hand. "You're telling me that old, brittle, beanpole of a man did this to you? At least tell me he had henchmen."

"Well..."

"Black magic?"

"Umm..."

"A sword? A knife? A really frightening feather?" Willuna tilted her head to one side, considering the farmer. "You put the rope around yourself, didn't you?"

"He was really quite convincing!" The farmer craned his head around as he slowly twisted in the air. "He had this whole sad story about-"

"Don't care."

"Oh. Well. At least he didn't get me to hang myself, so kudos to me, right? I don't suppose I could ask you for the kindness of gently-"

The princess took three quick steps to where the rope, after passing over the branch overhead, was looped around the trunk of a thick tree. She pulled the rope loose of its knot. The farmer crashed to the ground.

"Thank you," he said, as he tried to get to his feet. Unfortunately his arms were completely asleep and just dangled at his sides like birds in a butcher shop's window. He finally got up and took a look around. "You're all alone?"

"I am now courageous and wise and perfectly capable of handling my own affairs, thank you very much."

"So you know that the Castle Owl is actually that way?" The farmer pointed out a direction that was very much not the direction that the princess had been walking.

"Of course I..." The farmer wasn't paying attention to her. The nerve! His finger was still out and pointed, but he was turning in a slow circle. "Excuse me, your princess was talking." He still paid her no mind. "What's wrong with you?"

Idwal scowled and shook his head. "There's something missing."

"I'll have my dresses and my handmaids and soon I'll have my husband. What could possibly be missing?"

"Does it seem quiet to you? I mean *especially* quiet? Peculiarly and exceptionally quiet?"

"We are in the middle of a forest, you silly-"

The farmer took her by the elbow.

"How dare you touch me?" said the princess. But then she forgot her anger. The farmer had guided her only a few footsteps along in the direction he had pointed out. They rounded the final bend in the forest and Owltown lay before them. It lay quiet. Completely quiet. It had stolen the hush of a graveyard. "Where is everyone?"

"Your Highness, I hope you won't think it too forward of me if I insist on escorting you back to the castle."

Willuna marched into the city, completely unafraid. Sure, it was unusually quiet, but this was her city after all. "Oh now you're worried about permission, you and your grabby hands."

"It was just your elbow!"

"It was a *princessly* elbow. Makes all the difference you know." They passed through the streets, seeing not a soul. Not even a dog or a cat. No birds passed by overhead.

They finally came within range of the walls of the castle. The princess shielded her eyes against the sun and spotted a guard standing at the top of the wall overhead. "You there!" she cried. "Tell my father that I've returned!"

The guard didn't move.

"You! Guard!"

Still nothing. The guard just stood there, looking out over the town.

But finally there was a noise. Something had shattered somewhere behind them in the town. It had sounded like someone had dropped a clay pot.

"Something's terribly wrong," said the farmer.

Willuna rolled her eyes. "Relax. You're with me. In my city. Nothing is going to harm me here, it's simply not allowed. You're perfectly safe." She turned her eyes back up to the wall. "Unlike a certain guard I could mention."

"There!"

Willuna spun around. The farmer was pointing back down into the city. Willuna squinted. "I don't see anything."

"The rooftops."

"What? A cat? Are cats too exciting for your boring little town?"

"It wasn't a cat."

"What else could it be? What else goes clambering around on rooftops?"

But there *was* something there. Something way down near the bottom of the city. Something moving incredibly fast, leaping from one rooftop to another. A tile slipped off of one of the roofs, smashing down to the ground below, making the same sound they had heard earlier.

It was too big for a cat. It didn't move like a cat. It was heading straight for them.

And there was more than one.

"I'll bet they know what's going on here," said Willuna. "They'll answer or they'll face me and my seriousness." She thrust out a royal finger. "You there!" she called.

The figure didn't answer. It just kept coming and coming.

"You know what?" said the farmer. "I think it's time we go."

"Go? We're not go-"

"Quick like bunnies."

The farmer grabbed the princess and slung her over his shoulder. He ran, huffing and puffing his way along the wall.

"Put me down!" said the princess.

The farmer spun around to get a look at the leaping figures behind them. The princess' feet scraped along the wall. "Watch what you're doing, you idiot!"

Whatever the farmer saw, it made him run all the faster. The princess couldn't lock her eyes on anything, the farmer was bouncing her up and down hard enough to make her teeth click. "My-eye-eye-eye fah-ah-ah-the-er-er-er is-s-s-s go-o-o-o-ing t-t-t-t-o k-k-k-k-ill you-ew-ew-ew!"

Behind them more tiles fell. Weather-vanes twanged.

And then they were running through the castle gates. The farmer skidded to a stop and put Willuna down.

"You!" said Willuna, shaking a finger in the farmer's face. "Oh, they're going to have to build a whole new dungeon just for you. Treating your princess like a potato sack, how dare..." Willuna realized the farmer was ignoring her. Again! She couldn't remember the last time she had been so angry (in fact the last time she had been this angry she had been six and her nanny had refused to get her a puppy. It hadn't mattered to the princess that the puppy already belonged to another little girl - she was the princess, she wanted something, she was supposed to get it, that's just how these things went).

Instead of quaking in fear at her wrath, the farmer went down to one knee. Well, that wasn't complete grovelling, but taking a knee was certainly better than his ignoring her completely. But then the farmer stood again. He had something in his fist. He turned over his hand and opened his fingers. Laying on his palm was part of a small stone statue of a bird in flight. It seemed a pity that it had been broken, someone had done an excellent job in the carving.

The farmer pointed past her.

Willuna turned, and her eyes went wide.

The courtyard of the castle was filled with stone statues. Statues of guards, statues of scrubbing boys. Maids, grooms, a squire, two knights. A dog, two cats. More broken birds. No people. No living animals. Just the statues.

"I was in a bit of a rush when I came through here last," said the farmer to her back, "but unless I'm entirely mistaken, these weren't here before, were they?"

"Maybe they were a gift?" said Willuna. "Maybe one of the other kings had them done as a present for my father. Or maybe one of the princes had them done as a way of wooing me. I do get a lot of gifts from admirers, you know. Although I have to say, there's no chance these are going to win me over. What would I do with a statue of the boy who cleans the manure from the stables?"

"Your Highness," said the farmer quietly, "I don't think these are just statues."

"What do you mean? Of course they're... Ilsa? Elsa?" Willuna had found the two statues at the edge of the courtyard. The two girls, her handmaidens, were looking back towards the fountain in the center. They were so lifelike. You could see every inch of terror in their faces. Their arms were raised to protect themselves from whatever they had seen coming. Willuna was starting to think the farmer was right.

Whatever had happened here, it seemed to have taken the whole castle. The whole town. Which meant...

"Daddy!"

Willuna lifted her skirts and sprinted into the castle, ignoring the farmer's call for her to wait.

CHAPTER 7

The statues were worse inside. The people were caught fleeing, knowing that something was coming for them. Idwal didn't know where he was going, and he'd lost sight of the princess. Her slippered feet made no noise in the hallways. The torches and braziers had long gone to ashes. What light managed to penetrate the gloom came through the open doors of rooms that had windows facing the sun. Idwal's mind had a hard time believing this was the happy bright home of King Torquil. The castle echoed now of nightmares.

He was in the castle proper, that much he knew. But he'd never been taken anywhere near the royal apartments. He sprinted one way, then another. In the back of his mind those things on the rooftops were drawing ever nearer. In this gloom they could be at the end of this very hall, or waiting behind one of the open doorways.

The princess' scream cut through the air.

Idwal followed the echoes, weaving through the statues. He found a heavy set of painted wooden doors, the Owl crest carved into the wood. He slipped through into a large waiting room, and from there through another single heavy door into a bedroom.

Willuna was crumpled on the floor, sobbing. Above her stood her father, now stone. In his hands was a map, more maps lay scattered across the bed and tables. Idwal reached out awkwardly to maybe pat the princess on the back, but then he thought maybe he shouldn't touch her again. Which was somewhat ridiculous, he realized, considering he had just hauled across half the city with her slung over his shoulder like a sack of wheat, but for whatever reason this now seemed too personal.

Instead he stepped back from the princess and shifted through the maps. "He was looking for you," he said.

"This is all my fault." The princess dug her fingers into her hair, clasping her head.

"Stop that. Your Highness," he added. "Did you turn all these people to stone? Is that some kind of special power that princesses have?"

The princess sniffed, rubbed at her eyes. "No," she said, her head drooping. "But-"

"Blame the ones who need blaming. For now, I think we should go."

"Go? Go where? This is my home."

"We'll find someone to take you to one of the other kingdoms. They'll take you in, won't they?"

"Yes. I suppose."

Willuna held out her hand. Idwal took it. And then just stood there.

"Well?" said the princess, looking up at him.

"Forgive me, your Highness. It seems there's something sharp sticking into my back."

***

A voice spoke from behind Idwal's ear, full of anger and ugly promises. "There will be something sharp sticking out of your front if you don't remove your hand from the princess."

Willuna's head snapped up at the sound of that voice. She sprang to her feet and rushed forward, causing the farmer a moment of panic, thinking she was attempting to skewer him. Instead she knocked him aside and threw herself into the big strong arms of a ridiculously handsome man.

"Anisim!" she cried. "I knew you'd come!"

Anisim waved his astonishingly large sword at Idwal. "Who is this?"

"Hm?" said Willuna, her face pressed to the young king's chest. "Oh, him. He's just some farmer."

"Oh," said Anisim, lowering his sword. He looked at Idwal with interest. "Not the turnip farmer? I heard about that. What was it, some kind of special fertilizer or-"

Willuna gasped. *Really?* Again with the turnip? Now, when she was vulnerable and most assuredly beautifully distraught? The farmer was like a rash that just refused to go away, the kind of rash that lesser people had. Willuna reached up and grabbed Anisim's strong chin between her fingers, tilting his head down so he was looking at her. "You wouldn't believe the adventures I've had! First I-"

But Anisim continued to address the farmer. "We'll need provisions and weapons. This way."

Anisim turned and strode out of the room, clearly expecting the others to follow. And they did. It was impossible not to, really. Anisim's commanding presence was like a magnet, drawing the others along behind him.

"We'll make for my kingdom," he said. "Not that any place seems particularly safe anymore." Anisim stopped, eyeing a statue of a guard. "But my soldiers are wary and on alert." Plan made, Anisim nodded to himself and started up again, eating up the ground in his long supremely manly strides.

Willuna was delighted with the idea. "I concur. I suppose I'll be there for quite a while, you having to avenge my father and everything. We'll just nip over to my room so I can pack and then-"

"No," said Anisim, "no packing. We head to the armory, then the kitchens, and then we leave."

"But-"

"Um," the farmer raised a hand as he scurried along after the king. "I don't suppose it would be alright if I just went home?"

"But Anisim-"

"Are you sure?" said Anisim to the farmer, ignoring her. "I can think of no safer place than the Castle Wolf."

"You can't just expect me to-"

"I'm sure. I mean, thank you very much for your kind offer, your Majesty, but back home I've got a girl that needs marrying and a field that needs plowing and there's not a statue to be found."

"As you wish," said the king. "But you'll help me get the princess to safety first?"

"Oh no," said Willuna, "we're probably better off alone."

"That's probably true," said the farmer.

"He's very clumsy."

"Well, I don't know about-"

"He knows nothing about fighting."

"That is definitely true."

"And he takes astonishingly liberties with my body."

Anisim skidded to a halt and looked down at the farmer. "Liberties?"

"Er..." said the farmer, squirming. "Oh look," he said, pointing, "the armory."

The king gave the farmer one last glance and then went on through. Inside were rows upon rows of swords and pikes and daggers and bows and all sorts of polished bits of armour. Willuna was excited, and felt a bit naughty. Her father had never allowed her in here. She grabbed up a broadsword that was nearly as long as she was. Grunting, she hauled it up. It was far too heavy for her and it dragged her around, the sword swinging her instead of the other way around.

"Shiny!" she said, giving the sword a weak swing that spun her right around on her feet. The farmer winced and shuffled back. "Honestly," said the princess, "is there anything you aren't afraid of?"

"Boredom and old age."

"Well you can have your silly blah vegetables and your silly little blah farm." The princess took another swing, shuffling along as the weight of the sword dragged her all over the place. "They'll sing of me for ages to come. Serious Willuna and her quest for vengeance."

"What are you doing with that?" Anisim strode over and grabbed the long sword away.

Idwal sang under his breath, "There was a young maiden of lore, who wasn't to play with a sword-"

The king rounded on him. "And you, you haven't armed yourself yet?"

"Me? Armed?"

Anisim grabbed a bow and a quiver of arrows from their stands and shoved them into the farmer's hands. The farmer looked ridiculous holding the weapons.

"I'm not a hunter."

"That's not a hunter's bow," said the king. "Now for the kitchens, then we're off."

And Anisim was off again with those manly strides, the others following along behind. Willuna watched as the farmer tried to sort himself out, slinging the quiver over his shoulder and trying not to trip on the bow.

"Please understand your Highness," said the farmer, "I'm not a soldier. I can't shoot, I can't fight, and a miser outwitted me. I'm a wretched failure at this adventuring business."

"It's true," said Willuna, "he is. We should leave him someplace and go on alone."

"Speaking of alone," said the farmer, "shouldn't you have guards? I thought important people always had all sorts of guards."

Anisim peered around a corner, making sure the next hallway was safe. "There was a hundred of us making a tour of my kingdom's inner posts. A messenger tracked us down and told us that Willuna's father was asking for help to find her."

Willuna beamed. This was more like it. Her handsome, gallant king dropping everything to ride in a search for his beautiful queen to be.

Anisim turned and looked down at the princess. "What were you thinking?"

"But I did it-"

"Onwards." Anisim started walking again, hand on the hilt of his sword. "Me and my hundred were nearing the crossroads that would lead us here when we came across a very cranky old gravedigger gibbering a foul tale of robbed graves and emptied tombs. And then the very next moment these... *things* hit us. They came pouring out of the woods, moving so fast... And even when one of us managed to hit them, they wouldn't go down. They wouldn't bleed. I swear I saw one lose a leg. It just stood on its hands and charged us again."

Willuna didn't want to hear this. What she wanted was to have Anisim to herself, all alone, where she could tell him how she had become a serious young lady and that it was alright for him to marry her now. She wanted Anisim to tell her that her father would somehow be okay, that this evil statue curse was no worse than a common cold and could be cured, abolished. And walking behind him, looking back over her shoulder, what she suddenly wanted most of all was to tell the other two that there was something moving in the shadows behind them.

"When it was over I was all that was left of my unit. My men, their bodies had been dragged off into the woods. All that was left of them was one empty helmet..."

"Um," said Willuna, pointing behind them. She was ignored.

"One helmet?" squeaked the farmer.

"One helmet," said the king, "rolling across the road. I'll never forget that sound."

"Yes, okay but-" said the princess again.

"All of them gone."

"Look at my finger!" said Willuna. And they did, finally.

"It's a very nice finger Willuna," said the king.

"As fine a finger as they come," agreed the farmer.

"Honestly?" said Willuna. "Look!" And she thrust her finger out again. Finally the two men looked back down the hall. They were coming, the things. Crawling over statues, along the walls, hanging from the carvings along the ceiling. Creeping and grinning. One of them made a tiny little tinkling noise.

"Oh," said the farmer.

"Ah," said the king.

"For my father," said the princess, "charge!"

But instead Anisim grabbed her around the waist and sprinted the other way.

"Why aren't we killing them?" wailed Willuna.

They barrelled into the kitchen. Anisim turned back. "Use your bow!" he said.

It took the farmer a moment to realize Anisim meant him. He'd never had a martial command directed at him before. "Oh! Me! Right!" he said. He fumbled around over his shoulder and managed to pull an arrow from his quiver, scattering three or four more across the floor. He turned, fit the arrow to the bow's string, and aimed back through the doorway. And loosed the arrow! Sort of. The arrow promptly dribbled over the farmer's fist and flopped down to the floor.

Willuna was far from surprised. "Well there you have it," she said.

The silent creatures continued to speed towards them. Idwal rushed forward and slammed shut the heavy wooden door. He ran over and huffed and grunted and strained, shoving a heavy table in front of the door.

"I want to go home, I want to go home," whined the farmer.

"Don't worry, Anisim will slay every last one of them."

The farmer's eyes were almost as adoring as hers as he looked up at Anisim. "Really?"

"Or die trying."

"I want to go home, I want to go home."

Anisim took up a stance that looked very deadly. He stood with his feet apart, his front arm pulled back, his rear arm crooked in a sharp angle. The sword swayed in the air, horizontal. It reminded Willuna of a jouster's lance. Those things out there were in for it now.

"Farmer," said Anisim, "get ready to throw open the door."

"Open the door?" The farmer's voice quivered.

"I'll do it," said Willuna, She put her back to the heavy table, ready to shove.

"No," said the king.

"I can do it!"

"I said no." Anisim stepped forward and grabbed Willuna's arm, pulling her back and shoving her out of the way. Willuna tripped on the hem of her dress and fell to the floor. "Now's not the time for your nonsense," said the king.

He hadn't even noticed Willuna's tumble. Willuna sat in a heap, shocked and hurt.

The shutters over the windows smashed in. Kindling flew. Pale hands burst in, clawing, groping. Fingers twisted into the farmer's shirt, Anisim whirled and hacked them away. Grinning faces started to squeeze through the narrow windows, mortis grins leading the way.

The princess had no trouble permitting the farmer to touch her this time. He yanked her up by her hand, the two of them stumbling to the back wall of the kitchen. The room was open, no corners to hide in, no nooks in which to disappear.

Anisim put himself between them and the intruders. "Trapped! Well come then fiends, and find the Wolf King ready!"

"Oh," said the farmer. He pointed past Willuna. "Couldn't we just go through there?"

Willuna turned to look. A long low slab of wood, like a door standing on its edge, was hooked to the wall by rails and pulleys.

"Certainly not," said Willuna, "that's the garbage chute."

Anisim called back over his shoulder. "Does it lead outside?"

"It leads *garbage* outside."

Anisim nodded to the farmer. Idwal reached up and yanked on the dangling chain. The door of the chute glided smoothly up, exposing a garbage-strewn hill outside.

"No," said Willuna. "Absolutely not. I am a princess, thank you very much, and I simply will not-"

Anisim shoved her through. Willuna went somersaulting down the hill, getting coated in garbage, layering herself in the smells of rotting beef, weeks old eggs, stuff and goo she couldn't even begin to identify. It was a good thing that all the tumbling and bumping and scraping kept knocking the breath out of her; the words she would have chosen to express just how much she hated the farmer at that moment wouldn't have been very princess-like at all.

And then the river appeared below. Getting closer. Churning white as it rushed by rocks. Willuna tried to dig her heels in, but the ground was slick with ooze. She clawed at the ground. Just as she was about to bump off into the water a hand reached out and grabbed her wrist. Willuna looked up past the rough grip and saw the farmer holding onto her with one of his dirty peasant hands, the other clinging to Anisim's leg. Anisim in turn, above them both, was hanging onto the pommel of his sword which he had driven, heroically of course, into the ground.

The jesters slipped by them. Reaching and groping, the lithe little creatures found no purchase and sailed off into the river, all of them going by with only one splash between them.

The jesters didn't resurface. Good. She wished them all the most miserable of drownings. And not having to fend off evil-doers would give the princess more time to really tear into the farmer. She got herself to her feet, slipping and sliding. She pointed at the farmer, her eyes nothing but fury, so angry she didn't know where to begin.

"Um," said the farmer, picking an apple peel off his forehead, "I don't suppose that's a finger of gratitude and thanks?"

"Gratitude?!" She poked him in the arm. "Thanks?!" She poked and poked again. The farmer scrambled back, the princess chasing after him across the slick ground. "Look at me! I'll give you thanks! Thank you!" Poke! "Oh thank you!" Jab! "Whatever would I have done without you?!" Slipping on bacon grease, the princess scrabbled across on her knees so she could beat her little fists against the famer's stupid peasant chest.

A woman's scream peeled out from the bottom of the hill. Anisim, who had been coming to the aid of the farmer, turned and slid his way down to the very bottom of the hill.

Instantly forgetting the farmer, Willuna turned and chased after him. "Don't leave me!' she called. The farmer tried to stand, slipped, and decided to crawl down the rest of the way.

At the very bottom of the hill they found a woman, the very same woman from the market who had given a coin to a poor beggar. She was frantically scrambling along the edge of the river. "My daughter!" she cried, pointing at the river. "She got knocked in by those… those *things!*"

The farmer jumped into the river, his stupid peasant bottom hitting the water first with a tremendous splash. Anisim stripped away his armour, fast as he could. Chest-plate off, greaves gone, boots kicked aside, he dove in, barely causing a ripple. They resurfaced downstream, blowing for air, and dove under again. And again. The two women hurried along the bank of the river, keeping up.

A few town-folk who had, one way or the other, dodged the statuesque fate of their fellow citizens, had come running at the sound of the woman's screams. Now they too hurried along the bank, searching for the little girl.

Too long, thought Willuna, it's been far too long.

But then the king surfaced, gasping, and in his arms was a limp little form. Eager hands pulled them both to the ground. Anisim laid the girl, no more than six or seven, out on the grass. She was beautiful, and you could tell that she, like a closed rose waiting until it was time to unfurl its petals, would have grown more beautiful still. But now her body was limp, her lips blue. They had been too late.

"Another crime those creatures will be made to answer for," said the king. He brushed the wet hair from the little girl's forehead. "Be at peace, little princess." He leaned down to give her a gentle kiss good-bye.

Willuna's heart broke at the sight. She spun around, unable to watch, bumping into Anisim's side. The bump caused Anisim to puff, the air forcing its way into the little girl's mouth.

The girl coughed water up into Anisim's face. Her eyes popped open.

"Hooray!" said the crowd. "Huzzah!"

"Thank you!" cried the mother, gathering the girl in her arms.

"His kiss is magic," swooned Willuna, her eyes full of the magnificent man before her.

And somewhere down the river the farmer called out, "We find her yet?" in an exhausted voice.

That was how Willuna first came to truly know tragedy. But it was also how she learned that there was always a reason to hope.

She also learned that she really wanted to start kissing Anisim. A lot.

CHAPTER 8

It took a special kind of castle to be truly foreboding. Stone alone scared no one. It took echoes in empty halls, rotting curtains billowing to escort in the rolling fogs. Cobwebs in corners were an absolute must.

Bodlomous was not yet satisfied with his home. He had jesters climbing every wall, clinging to every delicate chandelier, escorting spiders to their new homes, showing rats the hidey-holes with the grandest views.

"More festering!" he called out striding down one of the long dark halls. "I absolutely must have more festering! How are we ever going to have the proper company come to visit if everything is airy and bright?"

Rotter the jester came galloping down the hall, kicking up dust. His cap bells tinkled a rusty tune. He stopped, quivering, happy to be back in his dread lord's company, and dropped a cold something into his master's hand.

Bodolomous looked at the thing. It was a small statue of a bird, one wing broken off, the beak smashed. "My god," he said, "they were attacked by birds?"

The jester shook his head no no no. He reached out a crooked arm and tapped his jagged nail against the stone wall.

"Someone turned them all to stone?"

Yes yes yes.

"Turned to stone. Condemned to watch all they've built come tumbling down around them. Hundreds of years of being able to look nowhere else, until finally the rain washes away their eyes. So cruel, so cold, it's absolutely brilliant." And yet, in the pit of his stomach, Bodolomous felt a tremble.

He was supposed to be the Most Evil Man Alive, but to do something like this to another human being...

He stuck the bird bits into a pocket up his long black sleeves. "Who did this?" he asked. The jester shrugged. "Were any left alive?"

Yes and yes again. The jester stood back, curtsied most prettily.

"The princess is still alive? Was she there? Did you capture her?"

Yes and yes and no.

The wizard stomped his foot in anger and slapped Rotter. The jester's head, held on only by thread, went tumbling off into the corner. The body groped around, hands twitching. "Why not?" said Bodolomous.

The jester mimed it all out. Someone had been protecting her, shooting a bow and arrow. Was it a guard? No. A knight? No again. Are you... hoeing? Yes!

"No!" bellowed Bodolomous. "Not the farmer! Not *that* farmer! That hoeing had better be code for legions of knights. On horseback. Really big horses. Clidesdales. Because I swear to you if it was that turnip-digging..."

The jester joined his hands together, wiggling fingers, wiggling thumbs. Bodolomous looked to the wall. A puppet made of shadow twisted, turned, and became a wolf howling at a shadow moon.

"The King of Wolves? Well, that's certainly better, isn't it? Much more proper, having a king as your competition. Could hardly raise my head in public, evil public, if I kept getting bested by some hick fresh in from the fields. But a king, ha!"

Bodolomous turned and strode off down the hall. Rotter's hands found his head. He picked it up and hurried after the wizard. "The Wolf King, my nemesis. I will have the princess, oh yes. Over your dead and humiliated body. And then the world will know and fear my name!"

He turned the corner and called back over his shoulder. "Let's get some ghosts in here if we can, eh? Evil, people, think evil!"

That's how it occurred to Bodolomous that you're only as good as your competition.

***

The Castle Wolf was a place of business. It was stern, not pretty. Solid, not inviting. The blocks of its walls had been carved one at a time out of solid grey rock and been laid with the thought of keeping unwanted guests out, not inviting friendlier guests in. The Wolf kingdom was the last of the human kingdoms before the civilized world disappeared into the wildness of the goblins, orcs, harpies and all such other fiends. This was a place where everyone believed all of the old dark tales, or at least believed that even the most outlandish stories carried at least a kernel of truth at their core. This was a place where everyone always carried a weapon.

Claramond was walking her rounds. The Wolf Kingdom had long ago done away with the idea that only men could serve as soldiers. There was just too much ground to cover. Anyone of any age who was willing and able was allowed to take the tests and swear their oaths. There really weren't any damsels in distress to be found in those parts, practicality had far outstripped romance in this borderland.

Claramond would certainly be considered pretty by you and I, but there wasn't much about her that one would point to and call ladylike, especially not in any sense that Willuna would recognize. Her hair had been cut short to fit under her helmet, the skin of her hands was rough and calloused. There were scars here and there on her body, rewards from lessons learned the hard way. She did own a dress or two, but it had been a long time since she'd had any occasion to wear them.

She was making her usual rounds. She was a sentry of the castle itself, a position that showed she was found to be trustworthy and solid of character. It was something of an honour among Wolf soldiers, receiving a position like that, but Claramond had a not-so secret desire to get out where the real action was, patrolling the fogs that marked the border into the dark places of the world. You could only circle the same buildings so many times without getting a little bored. There wasn't even anyone for the sentries to talk to, Wolf soldiers had been spread so thin as of late that sentries now had to patrol solo, instead of with partners or groups.

Round and round she went. She wondered how many times she would have to make this sweep before she started wearing a groove in the ground. The carved stone of the ground was grey, the stone walls were grey, even the sky was overcast and dreary. Everything was the same as it ever was. Except for the scraping sound coming from the Family Wolf's tomb.

The entrance to the crypt was set to the very side of the castle's courtyard. A projection of stone stuck out from one of the walls of the keep, its entrance always closed by two thick and heavy wooden doors. A key was usually necessary to open the lock that dangled from a chain that went from the handle of one door to the other. There was only one such key, kept by the chief steward of the castle. Someone had bypassed the need to talk to the steward; the lock sat on the ground, bubbling and melted by some kind of powerful stinking acid.

Claramond instantly drew her sword. The Wolf Kingdom had never been the kind of place where people tried to pass off bad noises as "just the wind". Almost all of the time if something hinted at trouble then there was in fact trouble to be found.

Next to the entrance of the crypt was a heavy box, its body made of stone, its lid of wood. She opened the box and grabbed one of the torches lying stacked inside, lit it in a nearby brazier. She looked around to see if there was anyone else nearby to aid her, or at least to go and find her another guard, but like it always was as of late, the courtyard was empty. She decided she would just go to the bottom of the stairs and take a look around, but wouldn't head into the underground maze without backup. There was something going on, she had no doubt; she just didn't know if it was the kind of something she could handle on her own or not. She was, after all, a Wolf soldier, and there were no better trained fighters in the world. If it was just an especially daring grave-robber or two trying to take advantage of the lack of guards Claramond was sure she could handle them herself.

In she went. Her feet scraped against the cold stone stairs as she went down, one rough step at a time. She held the torch ahead of her, sword ready in the other hand. The stairs were tall but narrow, nobody could get past her without her seeing them. The air was damp and chilly here. She felt a bit sorry for all those past kings and queens who had been laid to rest here under all this stone. She was a farm-girl, and when her time came Claramond wanted to be laid out in the open , under green grass, beneath blue skies.

A heavy *thoom* echoed out from below. Claramond stopped. Listened. Looked back at the entrance where she could see nothing but the grey skies overhead. Claramond would never admit to being scared, not even to herself, but those clouds suddenly seemed sweet and inviting, soft in this hard place. She felt a bit of iron pride trickle out of her spine.

In that moment of waiting something ticked and tickled toward her out of the long dark belly of the crypt. The sound of a thousand beetles rushing toward her. She stepped back, stumbled on a hard stone stair. The noise was on her, around her... above her.

She thrust up the torch. From the ceiling above her faces with too-wide grins tilted down, laughing silently at her, moving like crabs up there on the stone. They rushed by her, carrying a burden between them. One moment they were there, stopping her heart, terrifying, and then they were gone out into the grey air. She hadn't thought to cry out.

She rushed up the stairs. No sign of the intruders. A stable-boy came dawdling out of the stables, carrying a saddle in need of repair. No, he hadn't seen anything. No, he hadn't heard anything. Yes, he would alert the other guards, fast fast fast!

Claramond returned back down into the quiet stone room under the castle and cast her torch around, this way and that. There were no foot-prints in the dust to show her where the intruders had been. Her hands shook, but her pride carried her forward.

The oldest kings and queens were laying closest to the entrance. The tomb had been expanded as the Family Wolf had reigned on. As she moved further into the cool of the tomb she travelled by generations.

And then she found it. The last closed casket had been opened, its heavy carved stone lid slid aside and dropped to the floor. That had been the booming sound. The carving of King Anisim's late father, as stern in stone as he had been in real life, had cracked in half. There was nothing inside the stone walls of the sarcophagus.

The late king's body had been stolen.

This was how, eventually, King Anisim would learn that someone was out to make this personal.

CHAPTER 9

They had found an inn. After all that had happened it seemed the warmest place in the world. By the time they had reached the little roadside village the sun had been well on its way down, and Idwal had feared they would have to sleep in the open, vulnerable and exposed.

Anisim had money and had purchased them all simple clothes. The clothes were so ordinary that Willuna had at first thought Anisim was buying them rags. Anisim had thrown his reeking armour off into the nearby woods. Alone as they were, he thought it best that they travel unknown, giving their enemy less chance to find them. Willuna had objected, of course - all the adoring people they were sure to meet would happily help them. Who were they to deny her people the chance to mingle with someone they held as beloved? Anisim had overridden her objections, putting the princess into a foul mood which she promptly directed at Idwal. Somehow, as always, this too was also his fault.

They had stopped just at the edge of the village and taken turns washing off the smell of their escape from the Castle Owl in a creek that ran close by. Willuna had chided the king, warning him not to peek. Idwal wasn't sure, but Willuna had sounded like maybe she wouldn't have minded the king stealing a glance or two.

So now the two men sat in the common room of the inn. Willuna had gone off upstairs to her room to "repair" her new dress, even though Idwal hadn't seen anything wrong with it.

Idwal let the everyday sounds soothe him. A healthy fire crackled in the fireplace. Men laughed over a game of darts. Mugs were knocked together as villagers wished each other good health and long lives. This place was normal, this place was good.

Anisim drained his mug, ignoring the heavy admiring stares from the women who worked and sat around the room. He pointed at Idwal's mug. "Another?"

"Oh, no thank you. One is my limit."

"So," said the king, "this turnip of yours. Just how big was it?"

"Bigger than a pony," said Idwal, blushing, "but not so big as a horse. May I say, I'm surprised a warrior, er, a general, well, what I mean is, a king-"

"I do have a lot of titles, don't I? But while we're travelling," he lowered his voice, "in disguise, I'd prefer it if we left off the 'Majesties' and 'Graces'. Anyway," Anisim sunk back into his chair and rubbed a hand over his face, "despite all the titles I've really only ever been one thing - my father's son."

"It's not what you wanted?"

"Now that you ask me, I don't think I was ever really allowed the time to want anything of my own. I can't remember if I had a childhood hero... isn't that strange? My father's lessons, you see; I can tell you who made a sword by the balance and feel of the thing, but I haven't the first idea of how to bake bread. Or how to paint a painting. Play a tune." The young king sighed. "It must be pleasant, the growing of turnips. Perhaps one day if I can put a stop to these gruesome robberies I'll take a farming lesson or two from you."

"I think you'd make a splendid farmer."

Anisim smiled. Some ladies off to Idwal's right nearly fainted away. "Really?" said the king.

"Oh absolutely. If nothing else we can use that ugly mug of yours to scare away the crows."

The king roared. Others around them turned to see what was so funny. They joined in Anisim's laughter too, even though they had no idea what the joke was about. Idwal was beginning to see it, why people thought so highly of the young king. Idwal wasn't yet ready to invite the king to take a peek at him while he was bathing, but he thought if he had been the kind of person who needed leading in battle, Anisim would be the person he would most like to have at the head of the charge.

The king wiped laughter from his eyes. "The joke wasn't even that funny, was it?" The king chuckled again. "I must be tired. So, what about you farmer? Is the grass greenest where you live? Do you have everything you've ever wanted?"

"I suppose all I've ever wanted is to not want anything." Idwal dropped his eyes to his half-empty mug. "My parents, you see, they had fought for the king, Torquil I mean and, well… They settled down, but I suppose some of that… fire? Is that the word? Whatever it was, I guess they still had it in their blood, and it never truly cooled down. Not all the way, anyway. So one year, when I was still very young, one year once the harvest had been brought in they sent me to a neighbour's for safekeeping and off they went. They said they would be back in a week."

"What happened to them?"

"An adventure, I suppose. A sally-forth. Never heard from them again."

"I'm sorry. And what about *your* blood, Idwal the farmer? Is it completely cool?"

"What? Me? Oh, ice cold, I assure you. Absolutely." Idwal ran his thumb around the lip of his mug. "Although, now that I think on it, maybe there's a chance, I mean ever so slight of course, that it might be nice to have a young maiden look up at a body with some of what the princess-"

And then the princess herself was there, standing over their table. "I look dreary," she sighed, obviously expecting the men to leap over themselves to prove her wrong. Truth be told, she didn't look dreary at all. She did, however, look very odd. She was scrubbed clean, skin pink and healthy, hair now completely lacking bits of suet and potato peels. So, all that was fine.

But her dress, her simple honest dress spun of good honest wool had been, for lack of a better word, decorated. She had found some flowers somewhere and poked their stems through the weave of her neckline. She seemed rather proud of the effect. But instead of looking like decoration it looked like she had just won a horse race. More flowers were speared through the wool here and there without balance or symmetry. It looked like someone had assaulted her with petunias.

Now before your go wagging your finger at the young lady, we should take a moment here to understand Willuna. Girls born of royal blood were bargaining chips, married off to cement relationships with other kingdoms. It had pretty much been Willuna's job to fish for compliments ever since she was a child. How many of you have been working since you were three? Being attractive had always been her life's work whether she'd liked it or not.

The problem was that she had always had a lot of help. People had dressed her, taught her how to move and what to say. There was barely a thought in her head that didn't come from someone else. Unfortunately all those assistants had recently ditched their princess in favour of being statues, so she was suddenly on her own. She was vain, yes. She was petty, certainly, and had an incorrect and unfavourable view of common people. She bounced from grief to joy to anger and back again in the blink of an eye. But it must be said that she was only trying as best as she knew how to get along in the accident of life, just like the rest of us.

Unfortunately it wasn't enough. Anisim rose, and Idwal could tell from Willuna's face that her joy rose with him. It was obvious that she thought she had finally gained the right kind of attention from her perfect man. But instead of complimenting her, the king brushed past her and strode over to happily greet three soldiers in Wolf coats of arms who had just made their weary way into the inn.

Idwal felt bad for the young woman as her shoulders slumped, making her flowers bob and jiggle. "What do I have to do?" she said, and dropped down into a chair.

"You look very, um, clean," tried Idwal, but the princess didn't even seem to hear him. She just stared at the table top, her head drooping down.

Anisim strode back, grave purpose in his step. Anisim the wistful young man had been replaced by Anisim the king. "There's been news from the Castle Wolf. It... they took... Suffice to say that I don't think it will be safe for you there anymore Willuna. Farmer, you must swear to me you'll watch over her."

"Him?" said Willuna.

"Me?" said Idwal.

"I have no choice but to return to the castle, but I won't bring Willuna into that danger. Its walls have been violated. Considering what happed at the Castle Owl, who knows what will happen next? No..." The king paused, rubbing his handsome chin while he thought. "Take her to that village of yours."

"I will if you say so," said Idwal, "but it is just a village. And barely that. There's no walls. No watchmen. We don't even lock our doors when we go out."

"Who would think to look for a princess there? Go quickly and quietly. Go with my thanks." The king shook hands with Idwal. "Good luck. She's your burden now."

Before Willuna could say another word the king was gone, out the door with his men. Hurt and abandoned, she turned and looked at Idwal with scathing contempt that he felt go right through his skin. "My champion," she said. "A useless peasant who was bested by a scarecrow of a miser. I feel so safe now."

Idwal had thought he was used to the princess' jibes, but before now he had thought it all somewhat impersonal, almost as if it was a royal's job to look down at her inferiors. But this latest salvo seemed all too personal, and much to Idwal's surprise, it hurt. He scraped back his chair and stood, staring down at his hands. "I guess we'd better get a good night's sleep," he said. "We've got a good long walk ahead of us tomorrow." Head hung low, he turned and walked away.

This is how Idwal learned that royals, for better or for worse, were human beings too.

CHAPTER 10

Everything was stupid. The dirt road was stupid. The sky was a stupid shade of blue. Stupid birds chirped stupid little songs out of their stupid little beaks. Everything was awful and nothing would ever be good again.

Willuna stomped on along ahead of Idwal. She refused to look at even the back of his stupid farmer head with its ridiculous tan that ended where his shirt began. Every so often the farmer would have to call out a left or a right turn at a crossroads because the princess had absolutely no idea where she was going.

The farmer had tried to start a conversation once or twice in that stuttering manner of his, all hesitant and weak. Anisim would never have sputtered; he would have decided that a particular cow was well worth talking about and launched off in a strong, manly conversation. This went on all morning, the princess stomping and the farmer muttering. Willuna was using just all of her being to radiate waves of hatred at the peasant but he kept trying to make small-talk. It was getting pretty tiring and the farmer was just too thick to pick up her psychic hate ripples. She supposed she could have just come out with the words and told him how much she despised his very existence, but she was a princess and her moods and feelings were supposed to be picked up on, not stated outright, that was just how the world worked. The farmer couldn't do *anything* right.

Stomping and grinding her teeth with her anger frothing blackly at the edges of her vision, the princess ran right into something that seemed at first to be a screeching rainbow. It was only after she had disentangled herself from what turned about to be an astounding amount of astonishingly coloured skirts that Willuna realized she had collided with an old woman.

The farmer rushed up. "Are you all right?"

"No," said Willuna, "as a matter of fact I-"

But the farmer moved past her and helped get the old woman to her feet. Unbelievable! Now even the common stock was ignoring her.

Idwal got a look at the old woman's face. "Oh, it's you," he said with surprise. He turned to Willuna, who was still on her behind on the ground, glaring daggers up at him. Daggers that were being ignored. "This is the dear lady I was telling your father about, the one who stayed-"

"Are you going to help me up or not?" Willuna stuck out her hand.

Idwal grabbed it and yanked her up to her feet, but he had already returned his attention back to the old woman. "Are you hurt?" he asked her, "Can we do anything for you?"

"Well," said the old woman, dusting off her skirts, "I wouldn't turn my nose up if you offered something to eat."

"Sorry," said Willuna, clearly not sorry at all, "we're all out. Come along farmer."

"Could we give you some money?" Idwal asked the old woman.

"I hope you mean *your* money," said Willuna.

The farmer gave the old woman a smile, then moved Willuna a bit away for a private conversation. "I don't have any money," he said. "Your friend the miser took all mine, remember?"

"How did he do that anyway?"

"Er, never mind. Are you going to help her or not?"

"Why should I?"

"Because she's an old woman-"

"Obviously."

"And she's in need. Oh! Plus, she's one of your subjects. Aren't you at all, what would you call it, obligated to help her out? To give in her time of need?"

"*You're* one of my subjects and I wouldn't bother to give you a disease, never mind my money."

"What would your father do? After all you are now, you know, the queen."

Talk of daddy hit home. He would've given the old bag some money. He probably would have given her the cloak off his back and a ride home on his horse. Willuna had never been able to make him understand that he couldn't save everyone. One had to sacrifice for the greater good. Still, perhaps just this one time.

"Alright," she said, "in my father's name." She turned away, much as the Miser had done, and dug out her three coins. She was just about to turn back with them but hid one away. They were hers after all.

She brushed past the farmer and thrust out her hand, proudly displaying her two coins. "Feast your eyes on this, old crone!"

The old woman blinked. The farmer blinked. Willuna took in all this blinking, deciding that "nonplussed" was the best word to describe it, and said, "What?"

"That's all you're going to give her?"

Willuna looked down at the coins in her hand. All? What did he mean *all*? It was two thirds of her earnings! "This is all I have," she said.

The farmer frowned. "You worked how many hours for that man?"

"I wanted to buy myself a new dress for Anisim to see me in. Isn't this enough?"

"Deary," said the old woman kindly, "that's not enough to buy the needle to sew the thread to make the dress."

"Why didn't you ask for more?" said the farmer.

"I didn't know!" Willuna burst into tears. Everything was so ridiculously difficult outside of the castle! "Here, take them," she sobbed, and shoved the coins into the old woman's hands. She then turned and slouched her way over to the side of the road where she slumped down onto a tree stump to have herself a good cry.

"Now dear, no need for all that. I'll tell you what - because of your kindness I will grant you two wishes, one for each of your coins."

"Yes, um," said the farmer in a doubtful voice, "that's very kind of you madam I'm sure-"

"Don't you 'madam' me! I can do it! I, for one, have been on an adventure or two and have picked up all sorts of tricks along the way." She turned to Willuna. "Come on then love, make a wish."

Willuna sobbed on. She flapped a hand at the old woman, clearly believing the old woman's talk to be nothing more than nonsense.

So the old woman turned to the farmer. "You then young sir, take the first wish so your lady can see the truth of the matter. Perhaps you could wish for your money back and more."

"Oh no, not me. I like many things much more than money. Let's see…" The farmer tapped a finger against his lip, dreaming about all the things a farmer would desire. Willuna figured she might be about to see a man have relations with a sheep. "Ah! I know!"

"That took you a bit of thinking," said the old woman.

"Well, as I told the… er. Friend, as I told our friend, I've never really wanted anything. But! Just these past few days I was in Owltown and saw a great many musicians making a great many people happy with their music. So that's what I wish for. A fiddle. A fiddle fine enough to cause anyone who hears it to kick up their heels."

"Grand music it is!" cried the old woman. She did the oddest wiggle, swinging her hips to and fro, and then reached a spindly hand up under her skirts in a most indecorous manner, and then voila! Magic! She pulled out a fiddle and bow. She passed them over to the farmer who stood with his mouth hanging open in shock.

"Well go on then!" said the crone.

"I... I... well, to be honest madam, I didn't think you could... The thing of it is, I don't know how to play. Not a note, not a lick."

The old woman flapped a dismissive hand. "Pft," she said, "details. I'm telling you, give it a whirl."

So he did. The farmer stuck the fiddle under his chin, then drew the bow across its strings. And just like that, he was playing. And playing well. Not just well... he was excellent. In fact, he was the very best fiddle player Willuna had ever heard. She was surprised to find her toe tapping. She was even more surprised to find her whole body lurching up and dancing a lively jig. She hadn't wanted to do anything but cry... why was she up and bouncing about? She commanded her limbs to stop, but it seemed even her own body was getting in on the whole ignoring her thing. She danced on, spinning and leaping and having a right old knees-up, right until the very last note.

"Astounding!" cried the farmer as Willuna collapsed in a heap back on her stump.

The old woman cackled. "And still one wish to go!"

Willuna waved a hand, completely willing to make a wish now. But of course she was ignored. She was panting, far too winded to speak. The old woman had her back to the princess, and of course the farmer was doing what he did best, act the part of an ignoramus.

"I... I..." said the farmer, completely fired up by all the possibilities. "There was this archery contest-"

"Say no more!" said the old woman, and wiggled her hips again. Down under her skirts she went, and this time her hands popped out with a bow and quiver of arrows. Even stretched out like she was, Willuna had a moment to shudder at the thought of where the old woman was getting all these things from.

A leaf was drifting down from a tree along the roadside, see-sawing its way to the earth as leaves are wont to do. The farmer spun, notched an arrow, and fired, all in one fantastically smooth flurry of motion. His arrow sliced neatly through the narrow leaf and sunk into the trunk of the tree.

The farmer rushed over to pull the arrow from the tree. Then he bent down and picked up the leaf from the road. He wiggled a finger through the hole left by the arrow.

"Shoot the wings off a fly with that," said the old woman.

"Amazing," said the farmer.

"Well," said the old woman, dusting off her hands after a job well done, "that should keep you going." She waved. "Until we meet again!" She started off down the road.

"Wait!" said Willuna, finally getting to her aching feet. "I'm ready for my wish!"

The old woman called back over her shoulder. "Sorry ducky, but I'm all out. Thanks for the coins! Good luck on your adventure! And oh," she pointed off the side of the road to where an old logging track could barely be picked out amongst the trees and brush, "you might want to try that way." With that, she was gone.

Willuna turned and glared at the farmer. Never mind him picking up her waves of hate, now she was sure she could just burn him alive with her fury. But the stupid twit was tapping a finger against his lip again.

"Should have asked her about the turnip," he said. "And why did she offer to give me wish money if she needed our money in the first place?" He gave his lip a couple of more thoughtful taps, then shrugged. He turned to Willuna with a smile and showed her his new toys. "Who's useless now?" he said.

That's how Willuna learned that she could be ignored by just about everyone and everything, if they really put their minds to it. It was a shocking and awful lesson.

She also learned that you can't make a stupid farmer's eyeballs explode from their sockets using only the surging power of your fury. Not quite so shocking a lesson, but still a fairly disappointing one.

CHAPTER 11

They followed the path the old woman had pointed out. Idwal wasn't sure this was a short-cut home, but the walk itself was pleasant enough. The branches laced together overhead like fingers forming a steeple, cooling the unclouded sun overhead. The leaves shifted, a breeze found its way around the trunks, squirrels made happy sounds around them. It was a relief to know that there was a normal place or two still standing in the world.

Unfortunately the normality didn't last very long. Not half an hour after they started in they came across a small lane that cut through the trees to their left. At the end of the lane was a dappled clearing, and in that clearing stood a house.

"What is it?" asked the princess, wondering why'd they stopped.

"A house," replied Idwal. "A very short house. I mean, it looks rather well-built, the stone walls and all, but it must be awfully uncomfortable. The poor lumberjacks must have to hunch over all the time in there."

"Or maybe it belongs to dwarves."

"Dwarves?" The house no longer seemed even remotely appealing. Dwarves were not usually found in these parts. They were not usually found in forests in general, they tended to like things substantially more rocky. Dwarves were just not usual, in general. Why couldn't things stay normal for more than half an hour at a time?

The princess however seemed suddenly happy to have found the creatures. "Well bless that old woman's baggy wrinkles," she said. "She sent us right to fairy folk."

"Isn't that a bad thing? Don't they steal babies and make soup out of the bones of men and do all sorts of other generally rotten things?"

"What? No. Why would you possibly think that? Never mind, I don't really care. My father was very good friends with the short ugly brutes. Well, with some of them anyway, they have their bad sorts just like we do. But I'll bet these are the good kind."

"How can you tell? Just by looking at their house?"

"No, I just have a feeling. And your old woman sent us to them, so they can't be all that awful."

"You don't know that. The old woman just pointed at the path."

But the princess was already heading toward the house. "This is a blessing. You'll see. I should know, I've always been blessed - my beauty, my compassion... I'm on solid ground here. Things are finally going our way. Fairy folk always know about all the bad stuff that's going on."

"Well *I'd* know about all the robberies going on if I was the one doing all the robbing."

"I don't mean the dwarves were committing the robberies. Fairy-folk just... they always just seem to know things. I had an elven tutor growing up. She was the only elf I ever saw who got grey hair... Anyway, the magician is no fairy, and those were his minions that attacked us at the castle. I'm hoping the dwarves will be able to tell us where to find the magician."

"Find?"

"And then we can go capture him."

"*Capture?*"

"And then we present the magician, all tied up and defeated, to Anisim. Anisim is duly impressed, sees me for the serious woman I now am, and marries me. Then it's tra la la happily ever after."

Coming to the end of the path the princess suddenly darted behind the nearby bushes.

"What's-"

Her hand darted out and dragged him in after her. "Ick," she said, "they're hideous."

Idwal peeked through the bushes. Seven stumpy fellows stood in the clearing, heads bowed as they stood around something between them. Idwal wouldn't have gone so far as hideous, but on the other hand they weren't exactly the most visually appealing creatures on the planet either. They had all the features of regular men, they just appeared to have had someone lay their hand flat on the tops of their heads and push down, squashing everything underneath. They were as wide as they were tall, the lot of them strong with a worker's hard-earned muscles. If Idwal ever decided to compete in something, which was less than likely, he certainly wouldn't want to take on one of the dwarves in an arm-wrestling match. They looked human enough, but were distorted enough to make Idwal feel uncomfortable in their presence.

"Go talk to them," said the princess.

"What? Me? Oh no-"

The princess grabbed up a pointy stick from the ground and jabbed it into Idwal's bottom. He yelped and jumped up, right through the screen of bushes into the clearing. Seven pairs of distrusting eyes turned to him.

"Hello," said Idwal, trying his best to look completely unlike anything that would be threatening to a dwarf. He removed his cap. "I don't mean to be a bother, but-"

"Ach, heard, did ya?" said one of the dwarves. Idwal couldn't actually figure out which one had spoken; six of them had beards thick as sheep's wool and he couldn't spot any lips moving. "Come to pay your respects eh?"

The dwarves parted. Behind them stood a stone bier, as well-decorated as any bit of wood-carving Idwal could remember seeing. On the bier was a casket made of glass. And in the basket was the most supremely beautiful young woman Idwal had ever seen. Her hair was a thick waving black. Her skin was clean and white. Her lips were the red of the best kind of apples. Her breasts, pushed up by her blue dress, almost made Idwal weep.

Idwal moved closer. "She's so beautiful. Really beautiful. I mean, well, this is easily and by far the most beautiful woman I've ever seen. Ever. In all the years I've been alive."

"Ha!"

All the heads turned to see Willuna stumbling her way out of the bushes, slapping at a twig that got stuck in the hem of her dress. She pushed her way past the farmer to look at the young woman in the casket. "Her?" the princess said. "She's alright, I guess, in a common sort of way. But I mean, honestly, who needs lips that red. And those..." the princess turned her head away and waved her hand over the general vicinity of the dead girl's chest, "I guarantee you the dress is doing at least half of the work there."

Idwal could see frowns starting to spread over the faces of the dwarves. He figured it would probably be best if he turned their attention away from the princess. "What happened to her?" he said.

One of the younger of the dwarves stepped forward. "Her step-mother wished herself to be known as the fairest in the land. And beautiful she was, by all accounts. But it's plain to see that there is none fairer anywhere than our poor Snow-Drop."

"Ha!" said the princess again. She turned away. For some odd reason the hem of her skirt rode up a bit, displaying what would be considered in some circles to be a daring bit of ankle. Idwal could almost hear her brain saying, "Feast on that!" He turned his eyes away as another dwarf, this one with grey in his beard, took up the story.

"The way we've got it figured, the old girl sent Snow-Drop out with one of her house's most trusted men. Guess he was supposed to kill Snow-Drop so there weren't no more competition. But the house man was taken with Snow-Drop, just as any man might be, and couldn't go through with the foul deed. He set her loose, and she eventually made her way to us. Happiest day of our lives." The dwarf noticed the princess' display. "Hey girly," he said, "your skinny ankle is showing. And what's wrong with your dress?"

"Oh!" said the princess angrily, stomping her little foot.

A third dwarf spoke up. "Somehow that wicked step-mother sniffed out dear Snow-Drop's whereabouts. As it turns out the step-mother was something of a witch, and she set her dark magics to a most wretched purpose."

Now it should be noted here that accounts of this bit of history vary. Snow-Drop was attacked, this much we know. It's the manner of the attacks that varies. Some of them get downright perverted, if you want to know the honest truth. One fails to see how the witch giving Snow-Drop an overly long massage involving honey and tickling could be considered a murder attempt. So we're going to go with some of the more likely stories.

The witch had disguised herself as an old woman, this much is consistent in all the histories. She had somehow, magically one assumes, transformed herself into a crone. So disguised, she had first come to the short stunted cabin claiming to be a poor merchant who was selling corset stays.

Snow-Drop, being a charitable soul, had bought some of the stays and had allowed the old woman to lace them into her corset. But the old woman had *really* laced them in, with her foot in Snow-Drop's back as she pulled as hard as she could. Snow-Drop's corset had tightened so much that she had been unable to breathe and had fainted. Fearing discovery, the evil step-mother had hurried away without making sure the job had been done.

By now Idwal had taken the trouble to learn the names of all the dwarves. So he knew it was Winfried who said, "It was only luck that we arrived back in time to loosen poor Snow-Drop's stays."

The princess was simply shocked. "You touched her underthings?"

"She was suffocating."

"Yes, but still!"

Idwal intervened. "But if you saved her, then why does she lie before us?"

"There was a second assault," said Cosimo. "Got no idea how the witch learned her plan had failed, but she was soon back in another disguise."

"Wait a moment," said the princess. "If this wicked step-mother of yours has the power to change her looks with the wave of her hand, why didn't she just make herself more beautiful?" This got her no answers, only a bunch of scowls. "Well I'm right, aren't I?"

Egon stepped shyly forward. "We warned our precious Snow-Drop to be cautious, but once again she traded with the crone, for she had a most soft and gentle heart."

"You think her *heart* was soft?" muttered the princess.

One has to assume that the wicked witch had somehow changed her disguise. But perhaps not all that much. Willuna was right, Snow-Drop may have been astonishingly lovely, just downright gorgeous, really, but she wasn't the sharpest knife to ever cut butter.

So the witch had come back, maybe this time with a patch over her eye. This time she had held out a shiny comb. Snow-Drop, with her thick dark hair that, quite frankly, any man would have killed to be able to run his hands through, had clapped her hands with delight. Unfortunately the reason the comb was so shiny was that it had been dipped in poison. The tines of the comb had been sharpened to fine points, and as Snow-Drop ran the comb through her hair the poisoned points had pricked her scalp. In went the poison, and down to the ground went Snow-Drop.

"Poisoned!" said Idwal.

"Oh don't worry," said Winfried, "we saved her again. But her step-mother once again somehow learned that our beloved Snow-Drop lived on, so one day-"

"Wait," said the princess, "are there many more of these?"

"Last one."

The princess flapped her hand… get on with it.

The poisoned apple is of course the bit that all historians agree on. Long story short - the crone, now maybe with the patch on the other eye, offered Snow-Drop the poisoned apple. Snow-Drop clapped her hands at the apple. Snow-Drop bit the apple. Snow-Drop hit the ground like a dropped sack of hammers.

Winfried carried on. "The poison on the apple was so great that this time we could not bring her back. And so…" He motioned sadly to the casket.

Dietwald ran a hand over the glass. "She breathes still, though oh so slowly."

"What?" said the princess, her eyes wide, "she's alive but you put her in a casket anyway?"

"So that all may come and lay eyes on her beauty," said Cosimo. "Besides, it's not like we buried her."

"Let me get all of this straight," said the princess. "You take her in, she lives all alone with the seven of you, um, men-like people..."

"Yes?" said Egon.

Idwal could see that this could lead to nothing and nowhere but trouble. He opened his mouth to remind the princess that they were there to get directions to the magician (well, truth be told, Idwal was there to hopefully find out that the dwarves had no idea where the magician was, and really just assuming that they would know because they had magic in their blood seemed kind of racist to him), but the princess waved a hand to command him to be silent.

"And each time you went off to work," continued the princess, "leaving no guard, the same crone came by and duped Snow-Dip here-"

"Snow-Drop," said Idwal.

"Whatever, the witch duped her over and over again with a shiny this and a glossy that, even though you warned her every time."

"Indeed," said Friedemann.

"Exactly," said Gerhard.

"You've got it," said Udo.

"Well," said the princess, mulling this over for a moment, "what a silly little twit. So! Would anyone here know anything about a really evil magi-"

***

Idwal and Willuna fled through the woods. Happily, dwarves are slow runners, what with those stumpy legs and all.

That's how Idwal learned that a certain princess could really haul ass if the occasion warranted.

CHAPTER 12

Sweat worked like ants under her dress, against her skin, tickling its way just everywhere. Willuna didn't care for sweating, it was both uncomfortable and unladylike. She had in the past perspired at the most during vigorous dances. But now she was drenched, hair plastered to her temples in whirls, clothes sticking to her body. An alarming thought - what if she smelled?

The farmer was standing hands on knees, gulping air like he wanted it all for himself. They'd run like, well, like seven very insulted dwarves were out for their hides. Willuna had had a good mind to turn around and inform them just who it was their were howling at, but then remembered Anisim wanted her to stay in disguise. So she'd reined in her temper and picked up her feet. Eventually they had lost the dwarves and come to a gasping halt here by a farm's split-rail fence.

The farmer shuffled over and plunked down with his back to the fence. "I'm horrible," he said.

"I admit it could have gone better," said Willuna. "But I don't think they knew anything."

"I tried," he said, "I tried to bring myself to shoot."

Willuna looked over. The farmer sat slumped, his head bowed, not meeting her eyes. He was finally showing a person of her station the proper respect by not looking directly at her and yet, somehow, she felt bad. He just looked so sad.

"I don't mean I wanted to kill them, just frighten them a little, zing one through one of their hats. I could have done it too. But... but I just ran. I couldn't turn myself around."

"Well, what of it?" said Willuna. "I was running too. They were scary little men."

The farmer shook his head. "What did I think? That I would get this," he hefted the bow and its quiver of arrows, "and what, I would be brave? Strong? Be like King Anisim? You were right," he said, dropping the bow to the ground, "I am useless."

The farmer was absolutely the most annoying person Willuna had ever met. He was ignorant, a rube, far too familiar with his superiors. And now, on top of all that, he was making her feel sorry for him. And even worse, sorry for having made him feel bad.

Well, she wasn't having it. She was fine with looking down on him, trading words with him, she had even somewhat forgiven him for the slide down the garbage hill (even if Anisim had been the one who actually pushed her down, it was still entirely the farmer's fault for having suggested it in the first place). But feel sorry for this commoner? Absolutely not.

"Get up," she commanded. "I know this place." She looked around. "I think. We need to go."

"Go where? Pardon me your Highness, but why- "

"Because," she said, "it's time for another lesson."

That's how Willuna learned that insults don't always just hurt the one who is insulted.

***

The sun beamed down, straight, locking away shadows for the noon hour. It left nowhere for Idwal to hide his shame. It was now his turn to trudge, to drag heels, to set his pace to the speed of his mope.

The princess wasn't getting them anywhere particular in a hurry. She'd call out that she knew this rock, no, but she recognized this fence, wait and wait again, this lane was it, she was absolutely sure. They twisted and turned and recovered their own tracks like weathervanes in a tornado.

But then, suddenly, aha! Here it was! Idwal looked up from his feet to see exactly what was here, and saw a depressing, lurching house in front of him. Although, he had to admit, the windows looked exceptionally clean.

"Down!" said the princess, and dragged him into hunch behind a rickety fence that was missing pickets.

"Look!" said the princess, and stabbed out a royal finger.

It was the Miser. He was out towards the back of his house, shaking a sharp fist at something in a tree.

"This is *his* house?" said Idwal. "You brought me to the house of that... that nogoodnick? I don't have any more money to give him."

"He wronged you. My subject. In my kingdom. I am the queen now. I won't have purses snatched under my watch. He robbed me too you know. Of my time, and my lessons, of my chance to become serious and courageous and wise. Of my chance to become the perfect queen to the perfect king. I want revenge, you want revenge, it's time for revenge."

"What are you going to do?"

"Me? I'm going to walk right up to him and demand satisfaction."

"Pardon me, your Majesty, but I don't know that that's much of a plan. It's a bit bare of threads, if you will. And he nearly got me to hang myself. Who knows what he might do?"

"Who knows indeed? But that's my plan. So unless you can come up with something better..." The princess stood and started forward. "Oh, here I go, all threadbare and vulnerable. Oh who knows what foul fate might befall me. Oh oh oh..."

"Wait!"

"Have you thought up something else?"

"I..." Up until then Idwal's world had been plotted out by seasons and seeds and ancient farming wisdom. There had never really been a need to come up with a plan on his own. But now the princess was at risk. So come up with a plan he did.

This was how Idwal learned that necessity was a mother.

Of invention, that is.

***

If you asked the Miser if this story was about him he'd charge you $2.50. And he'd probably get it from you too. He'd been swimming downstream for some time now, ever since he'd met that empty-headed girl at the market. A pretty ornament to be sure, but in the Miser's considerable opinion, her light was all on the outside, not much shining out from behind her eyes. He'd worked her like a mule, and pretty much paid her like he'd pay a mule too.

Then there'd been the rube with that amazing amount of money. He'd cut across the farm boy's path and told him that he, an old fragile man, was being threatened by that rope on the ground. As the farmer had gone to pick up the rope the Miser had screeched at him not to touch it! It's a wicked rope! Simply full of ropely evil! Whatever you do, don't step inside of its circle of devilish ropery! And of course the hick, being overly full of good thoughts and the desire to be helpful, had done just that to prove to the Miser that he was perfectly safe. The Miser had gone over to the tree where the other end of the rope, after looping over the branch overhead, was tied to the harness of a mule (an actual mule, not a girl who just worked like one). Miser slapped mule's rump, mule hee-hawed and trotted forward, rope tightened around country bumpkin. Simple as that. He'd actually been hoping for the rope to squeeze itself around the country boy's neck, but he wasn't sure the farmer was quite stupid enough to fall for the same trick twice, so he contented himself with leaving the farmer dangling. He'd tied the rope off around the tree and picked up a stick which he used to poke at the farmer until the farmer shook the bag of coins loose. A fine day's work that.

As if he wasn't blessed enough, now there was this squirrel in his own back yard. As fine a squirrel that ever squirreled a nut. It was the colour of spun gold, from nose to tip of its tail, and the Miser simply had to have it. It was obviously meant to be his. People would pay to see such a thing. If not, the pelt must be worth a coin or two.

He deserved his good fortune. 'Course he did. Came after a life-time of fighting off vultures and harpies always dipping their claws into his pockets. A man could only fight the good fight for so long without getting tired. Without the world slipping in a little reward.

Speaking of vultures, two of them were hobbling toward him right that moment. Puffy folk. Fat. Didn't lack for food, these two, so why'd they want to bother him? Faces kind of familiar, not that he cared. Dirty. Which meant unrefined, which meant empty pockets, which meant the Miser couldn't be bothered giving them the time of day. He'd hurry them along double-quick, then get back to his golden game.

"You all right there lovie?" said the woman of the pair, her voice a ridiculous croak.

"Fine. I'm fine. Quite fine. Thanks for stopping by."

Drats. The woman had spotted the golden squirrel up in the tree, sending down angry chitters to patter against the top of the Miser's bald head.

"Well lookee that," she said. "Never seen one that colour before. Looks spun of gold."

"Could be he's valuable," said the dirty man. "People'd pay to see the likes of him."

"No!" said the Miser. "I mean, no, I doubt it. I'm sure of it. No. Well, good day to you then." The Miser sketched what might be called a bow by the more generous amongst us, then took a step away. Waited for the dirty people to move off. But they didn't. He stepped back. "Bye." And he stepped away again. Took another step. But the dirty people took hints about as well as they seemed to take baths.

The Miser stepped back and sighed. Fine, if he couldn't get rid of them maybe he could make use of them. That's what a smart man would do. Make something out of nothing. The dirty fellow had a bow and bunch of arrows. The Miser, having no experience with weapons, decided that maybe the dirty people were more good and well-deserved luck fallen into his lap. "Right," he said. "You. I'll pay you a whole copper coin if you use that bow of yours to procure that creature for me."

The Miser grinned as the dirty man stood up straight. "You hear that wife?" said the dirty man.

"Wife?" said the dirty woman, frowning.

"A whole copper coin!" said the dirty man. "No more eating the children. Huzzah!" He leaned over to the Miser. "Good thing the wife's been blessed with them sturdy child-bearing hips eh?"

The dirty woman sneered. "Oh husband," she croaked, "we're rich! We can finally get that vegetable patch! Plant all those exciting turnips-"

By now the Miser had rolled his eyes three times. He felt like he was stepping into the middle of an argument. He additionally felt like he didn't care. All he wanted was that money-making rodent in the tree. "Today would be my preference," he said.

The dirty twits stopped making faces at each other. The man got his bow ready. Then, for some odd reason, the Miser saw the man wink at the squirrel above. Maybe it was a hunting thing the Miser had never known about. Perhaps hunters all over the world were winking right now at deer and rabbits.

The dirty man let an arrow fly. It flew straight, cutting through the branch that squirrel was dancing on. The squirrel fell to the ground, landing on a pile of old leaves that had collected at the base of the tree the previous winter. The squirrel got up on its hind feet, its front paws clapped in front of its little squirrel heart in its final moments of woe. It staggered left. It staggered right. And then it stumbled right into the middle of a thorn bush.

"Don't let it get away!" cried the Miser, and he dove in after the critter. "Catch him!"

"I think not, you wicked man!"

The Miser stopped his scrambling. The woman had lost her screech. And sounded familiar, if no less unimportant. He tried to turn back to look, but his clothing was caught up on the little thorns. He settled for turning his head.

The dirty couple were shedding their clothes which, it turned out, were old burlap sacks. Stuffed with straw. And underneath all that…

"You!" said the Miser, "I know you! You're my house wench." He turned his eyes to the man. "And you're that fool that I had hang himself from a tree."

"Wench?" said the girl, completely indignant.

"Fool?" said the young man, completely considering. "Actually you might have a point there."

"Well you'll not have it!" screeched the Miser, thrashing around. He couldn't free himself from the thorns. "The squirrel is mine!"

The girl put her hands on her hips. "You know what would make this grand day all the grander, oh 'husband' of mine? A bit of music. Something one can tap one's toes to."

"Right you are!" said the man. "I knew there was a reason I married you. Give us a kiss then."

"Play your fiddle."

"Right you are!"

The Miser hated music. It got in the way; people dancing were people not making him money. He *really* hated *this* music. It was so happy, with no good reason at all. And yet he found himself up, as best he could in the thorns, and dancing around. And he couldn't stop! His feet kicked. His knees pumped. His elbows jabbed and his arms went swinging this way and that. The thorns danced right along with him, marking time through his clothes, making notes on his skin.

"What manner of sorcery is this?" he screeched. "Stop! I demand that you stop! I'll have you run from this place! From this kingdom! I'll have the king after you, we're the very best of friends!"

"Ha!" said the girl.

"I'll have you flayed! I'll have you swing! I'll have you catapulted all the way to the fairy lands!"

"We'll have my friend's sack of coins back."

It wasn't much of a fight. The Miser pulled the sack of coins from under his belt, clung to them as tight as he could. They were his. His! By right of being craftier than the country bumpkin. By right of being smarter. By right of the fact that the world would be a completely unfair place if someone who would actually walk into a rope trap on purpose possessed such a treasure. But oh, those thorns!

He threw the coins right at the young woman's feet. As she picked them up the young man finished his tune with a flourish. The Miser collapsed. His nakedness was covered more by scraps of cloth clinging to the thorns around him than by anything that could be considered clothing anymore. The squirrel darted in and bit him on the nose.

He watched the young couple walk away, smiling and happy with their evil deeds. The young woman passed over the sack, telling the young man how her father would be proud of him and that he wasn't quite so useless after all. Whatever that meant. "Not bad farmer," she said, smiling at her cohort, "not bad at all."

That was how the Miser learned that if you're going to leave someone hanging from a rope, it really is worth it to make sure the rope is around their neck. Half measures weren't going to cut it.

He also learned that the young man who had humiliated him was a farmer.

And finally, he learned that he valued revenge almost as much as gold.

Almost.

CHAPTER 13

They returned to Owltown that night. The princess' twists and turns earlier that morning had eaten up a big slice of the day, and the farmer seemed sure that they couldn't make his village by nightfall. But they certainly weren't going to stay in the castle with all those statues, so they went back to Owltown and settled on a good clean inn that sat near the river.

Dusk patted down the day, hushing noises, calming merchants. Heads that had heard of the curse up at the castle were poking out, cautious, stuffy from being inside all day with their fear trapped up with them behind the shutters. No curse came down with a breath of the thick evening air, only the scents of lilacs. One laugh was ventured, another town person answered with a guffaw. The town was daring to breathe again, expelling its terror to be forgotten in the dusk.

Inside the inn the crowd downstairs was getting up a ruckus, singing and drinking away the scary stories that had been filtering downward from the castle's walls. It was far noisier than Idwal usually cared for, but tonight in his heart he called for them to sing on and sing loud, because he too was happy to be alive.

He went through the door to the princess' room.

"Naked!"

And rushed right out again, blushing beet red. "Sorry!" he said. "Sorry! What were you-"

The princess called out from the other side. "Pulling hay from where it itches, that's what! This isn't the country, I'm not in a stable!"

"I know! I know it! I said I'd just be gone the one short moment, I... Here!" He thrust his hand back into the room.

"Soap!" The bar was snatched from his hand. "I had the innkeeper draw a bath for you. It's just down the hall. The world always weighs a little less after a good wash. Or so my mother used to say. So, um... right."

He about-faced, ready to march.

"Oh farmer?"

"Yes?"

"You were good today. Very useful."

"Oh. Well... cheers. My Lady."

He double-timed to his own room. Snugged the door shut, and gave himself a pinch. "'Cheers', he says, bravo. Not at all awkward or clumsy."

He threw open the shutters, demanding a breeze to cool his face. Down below a little girl, the very same one who almost drowned, ran and skipped around her mother, laughing. Her mother finally whisked her up and carried the giggler inside the house across the way.

Beyond was the river. The type of river that was full of water, water being the stuff that the princess was probably sliding into right that moment to work the soap along her skin... He imagined her sniffing the soap and smiling. He imagined the water steaming, causing beads of sweat to dance down her forehead, out along her small nose.

He imagined he could really use a distraction.

Then he heard her humming.

***

She had a voice as lovely as the rest of her. As the princess bathed, and yes, smiled, she hummed a pretty little tune. It twisted and spiralled through the air like a length of silk left out in an easy breeze.

Down through the inn's common room, quieting the town folk. Heads turned, ears pricked. Some eyes teared up. Memories travelled back to childhood when a mother's promise that everything would be all right was all that was needed.

The tune carried through the inn's door, out the windows, carried by the town to its children as a blessing. Young couples stopped, telling each other to listen, the melody explaining to each other all they felt.

The lamplighter stopped in his rounds. The lamps could wait for just a moment, light wasn't needed right away.

The notes tumbled into the house across the way. The mother sat behind the little girl, brushing out her long hair. Here too the lovely voice was explaining how a mother loved her daughter, all the more for almost having lost her.

The girl smiled into the mirror before her so her mother could see.

The mirror smiled back.

***

The tune had lulled Idwal to the bed. He had laid back, arms behind his head, eyes slowly closing. Like so many others, the princess' voice had wrapped him up in the promises his own mother had made, so many years ago. The humming soothed and patted and promised that the sun would come up tomorrow, same as always, that he would grow a little more and grow a little better. It hinted of how good he could become if he only tried, and that if he stumbled along the way there would be someone to pick him up again. It had been a very long time since Idwal had heard a promise like that.

But then came the scream.

The promises were cut away. Idwal snapped awake, alert. Out slammed the shutters, up whisked the sash. The streets below scrambled. Terrified town folk collided, bounced away, ran into another, nobody getting any decent fleeing done.

"What's wrong?" called down Idwal, but nobody was in the mood to answer.

Then the little girl and her mother joined the mess, either seeking shelter or seeking a way out, gaining neither. "The mirror!" screamed the little girl, her piping voice darting up through the din. "The mirror!"

"The mirror?" Idwal leaned out further, teetering. "What mirror?"

He looked up and saw that the rooftops were busy with devils.

***

Willuna had just stepped out from the greatest bath she'd ever had. She was patting herself dry when the first noises reached her. The shutters closed, the walls and door thick, she assumed it was just more celebrating.

But then a pounding at the door made her jump. She wrapped herself in the towel and opened it a crack, peeked out. The farmer shoved the rest of her clothes at her. With him came the sound of screaming, and there was no celebration in the voices. "What's going-"

"Quick!" said the farmer. "They've come again." The farmer did a double-take. The princess was standing there all glistening wet and showing an astonishing amount of leg. Willuna grabbed the clothes and shoved on the door.

A scream burst out from a door just down the hall. Scratches tickled their way across the roof - something nimble was crossing.

The farmer grabbed her wrist. "No time," he whispered and pulled her into the hall. He ran her to the stairs. Thirty different screams erupted down below.

The farmer turned them, dashed into the princess' bedroom. Slammed shut the door. Threw open the closet, dove under the bed, peered behind the big standing mirror. "All clear," he said. "Get dressed. I'm going to check to see if we can get out downstairs."

He stepped out, turned back. It really was just an awful lot of fantastic leg showing there. This time she did manage to slam the door in his face.

She backed up, clinging her clothes to her. Screams crawled in under the door, through the cracks in the shutters. It sounded like the whole world was nothing but terror.

"Horrible, isn't it?" said the magician.

***

His minions had lost her for a time. There'd been a lot of convoluted miming from Rotter, and a whole legion of jesters who had returned from the castle reeking of garbage. After that, she had vanished. He'd snuck a look into all of the human castles - Owl, Bear, Wolf, Badger, on and on, until his eyes had grown sore and his temper even worse.

Then he'd begun to check the towns and villages, spiralling out from the Castle Owl. But she'd vanished, she was vapour, she'd been hidden where his magics couldn't see.

He'd had his minions watching every bedroom, every dressing room, every castle and every stable that he had a set of eyes for. And as they watched he'd built more watchers, sewing limbs, planting heads. Tonight they'd found her, pulling hay from her dress.

He'd sent his minions out ahead. "Stir the pot!" he cried after them. "Scare children! Frighten women! Make cats climb trees and send the dogs running for the hills! Tonight is my night! Forever after, whenever the princess has a nightmare, it will be my face she sees."

And then, from his lonely castle half a world away, he'd stepped into her room, making sure his dark cloak swirled just so.

"The screams of women and children..." he said, and then stopped, eyeing the princess up and down. "Hey, you're all naked and wet."

The princess cinched her towel tighter. "If you were any sort of gentleman you would turn your back."

"Right. Sorry." Turn his back he did, but then he turned right back again. "Hey! Evil here! Show me some goodies."

"How dare you! You made a serious mistake, coming for me."

"Really? What are you going to do? Curtsey me to death?"

"I am Princess Willuna of the Fam-"

There were a lot of things Bodolomous considered saying at just this moment. Threats. Promises. Revelations of his own dark past. But in the end, sick of this condescending girl who didn't have the decency to be the tiniest bit afraid in his chilling presence, he went with a classic. He lunged at her and went, "Boo!"

The princess screamed and stumbled back into the corner of the room. Her arms flew up to cover her eyes. He had done it! He had impressed the princess! Oh glory be, oh happy day! Let her ignore him now, let her try to deny that he had made an impression. He had made *the* impression, the one that would linger with her for the rest of her life. He truly was the Most Evil Man Alive.

A fist flew in, nearly knocking the wizard's brain clear of his head. Bodolomous stumbled away from the princess, feet tangling in the hem of his robe. Fists bunched up the front of his robe and he was hauled to his feet. He was face to face with the farmer.

"You!" said the farmer.

"You!" said the wizard.

The farmer hauled back and laid in another one. The magician's vision flashed white, then black as his head thumped against the wall. His victory! His sweet victory! It was being pummelled out of him by the dirty hick! The nobody!

"No!" he said as he was boxed around the ears.

"Stop!" he whimpered as the breath was punched form his belly.

"Please!" he cried as he was thrown against the wall.

It was *ruined*. It was all ruined. He'd had it all in his hands, all he'd wanted, for only seconds. It wasn't enough. It wasn't fair.

"You!" he said, jabbing out a finger at the farmer. "I won! Look at her! I won, I tell you!"

The farmer stood above him, blocking the wizard's view of the princess. "Yes, you certainly do sound like a winner, what with all the snivelling and sobbing. Never seen anybody so happy."

And the wizard found he was crying.

Because of a simple, nothing, nobody farmer.

He'd been about to leave, to take his victory with him off to his dark castle. But now he'd be going empty-handed. The farmer had robbed him.

With that thievery, whatever little bit of the boy who, long ago, had fallen in love with magic and how it could make people wonder and feel awe, died away in his heart. What was left was a monster, and after this acknowledgement from one mere girl would never be enough for it.

His face twisted, ugly, full of hate. "I will have vengeance. When I come again, I will tear your worlds apart."

The farmer reached for him. Bodolomous thrust out his hands. Smoke, black as the deepest pit of the deepest cave, shot out like a squid's ink and clouded the room. The farmer tried to reach him through the smoke, but the wizard was gone without a sound.

The farmer managed to find the window and throw open the shutters. Waving out the smoke, he turned down and laid a hand on the princess' arm.

"No!" she cried, "Don't hurt me!"

He knelt down beside her. "It's me, it's Idwal. He's gone. Did he do some black magic to you?"

"No," said the princess, her head still down in her arms.

"Did he punch you? Slap you?"

"No," she said again.

"Well are you hurt? What did he…"

The sound of rattling shutters, not far off, made the farmer stop and listen. More shutters were shaken, closer this time.

He slipped his hands under her arms, pulling her up. "Come on," he said, "we're not out of this yet."

This was how the Most Evil Man Alive learned he had not been nearly evil enough. But he felt confident that was an error he could easily fix.

CHAPTER 14

She knew now that she would never have Anisim. She wasn't worthy. The magician had stripped her naked, more so than if he had only torn away her towel, and what was underneath was a coward. A coward could never be Anisim's queen.

Willuna let the farmer guide her down the stairs into the main room. The room was empty, meals left unfinished, chairs overturned. The fire was crackling down, smaller and smaller, in the fireplace. The farmer stopped her, ran over and opened the front door. Shutters were smashed in in the rooms above them. The farmer returned to her and they ducked down to hide behind the bar just before that horrible ticking sound signalled the arrival of the jesters. They followed with their ears as the soft rustling of cloth moved left to right, from the bottom of the stairs out through the open door. The farmer's ruse had worked, the jesters had passed them by.

Willuna sat limp beside the farmer as he peeked over the top of the bar. She started to pull on her clothes, not caring what the farmer saw of her. Her beauty was the only thing she had left, might as well share it.

The farmer checked out the door. Coast clear, time to get while the getting was good. He hurried back behind the bar, grabbed up Willuna, and out they went.

The collective scream of the town folk raised the hair on the back of their necks. It was like there were beasts circling, caging them in. A roar cut off the left, a wail cut off the right. The farmer sprinted ahead, sliding between two buildings, dragging Willuna along in his wake.

"There!" The farmer pointed. A rowboat was tied to a post at the end of the dock just ahead, bobbing stupidly as the current played with its frame.

"Above!"

Willuna looked up. Long twig fingers were wrapping themselves around the edge of the roof above them. A jester popped its head over, grinning its joyless slit of a smile down at them.

"Run!" The farmer jerked her along, head down, arms pumping, fear for fuel. Their feet skidded across dirt, then pounded wood as they made the dock.

Willuna looked back. Jesters were everywhere, too-wide smiles bright in the dark. She remembered herself, just yesterday, wanting to fight them all. Today she wanted to run, just as fast and as far as she could.

She ended up running right into the farmer, who had stopped to untie the boat. Into the river they went. The river was a feisty creature, rushing and bending like a kitten chasing after a ball of yarn. It bounced them off rocks and its banks and tumbled them head over heels. Between all this tossing and turning and slamming into boulders Willuna had a tremendously difficult time getting a decent breath into her lungs. On top of that her dress was doing a remarkable impression of a sponge, growing heavier by the moment and trying to drag her under. Through all of this Willuna could only think *I don't care, I don't care, I don't care.*

Still not caring, she felt the farmer latch a hand around her arm and drag her to the side of the river. Completely unimpressed, she felt more hands reach down and pull her out to stand shaking on the water's edge. Astonishingly underwhelmed, she heard the farmer gasp his thanks; and even when she heard the Miser reply that they were most welcome, Willuna remained fundamentally uninterested.

But then they were taking the farmer away. Now her head jerked up. The Miser had rounded up what Willuna supposed was some sort of hastily-formed militia. A bunch of burly men, they had the farmer by the scruff of his neck, his arms pinned behind his back, and they were marching him toward the city's central square. Much to her surprise, Willuna suddenly found herself caring, and caring very much at that. Her dreams were shattered, so be it, she would have to live or die with that loss. But the farmer still had his home to look forward to, and his girl, and Willuna suddenly felt very determined that *someone* in the midst of this whole mess was going to get what they wanted... and it most certainly was *not* going to be either a wicked magician or a foul-hearted miser.

She chased after them, trying to push her way through the trailing crowd. "Let me pass!"

The militia's leader, a squarish sort of man with a moustache that pointed out sideways like the wings of a bird stopped and looked back at her. "Who's this?" he asked the Miser, jerking his thumb back in her general direction.

"Nothing, a nobody," said the Miser. "Just the farmer's little crumpet."

"Oh now," said the militia leader, "no need to be degrading about it. She any sort of threat?"

The Miser eyed Willuna's oddly-decorated dress. "Her sense of fashion perhaps."

Willuna bristled. Insult after injury! "I will have you know that I am Princess Willuna of the Family Owl, and I demand that you unhand my friend, well, my acquaintance, well, my person who follows me around a lot, at once!"

The men of the militia and the Miser laughed and shuffled off, snickering about how a silly girl in a silly-looking dress could ever think such a ploy would work.

In the town square a gallows had risen, summoned up by frightened and angry hands. It wasn't all that impressive, as far as gallows went, looking as rickety and unsecure as the Miser's bones. The folk of Owltown hadn't ever had a reason to just throw up a platform meant to display death; add to that the confusion and fear that had its grip on their collective spine and, well, it wasn't their best work.

The Miser marched his little troop up onto the platform, steadying himself as the struts squeaked and swayed. "Good people!" he cried, gathering a crowd before him, "before you stands the man responsible for the horrors of this night!"

The farmer realized that the Miser had meant him. "Um," he said, "no I'm not." It wasn't the most persuasive defence.

"Don't be fooled," the Miser continued, "he may look the part of a simple, dimwitted rube. But where this man walks, danger follows!"

Willuna, trying to press her way through the crowd, realized that this was true. Because where the farmer had been walking, she had been walking too. Would the farmer have been chased by those horrible clown creatures if it hadn't been for her? Would the Miser have learned about the farmer's sack of coins? She stood on her tiptoes and saw that the militia men were slipping a hangman's noose around the farmer's neck. She couldn't let the farmer die because of his association with her. She stopped, wondering what Anisim would do in this situation, but she realized that was no help. She couldn't swing a sword like Anisim, or shoot a bow, and where was she going to get a hundred horses for a proper charge on such short notice? It didn't matter what Anisim would do - the real question was, what would Willuna do?

Well, she could undoubtedly use her beauty to enchant the men of the militia. They were all frightened and angry of course, but she was confident her radiant looks could win them over. But there just wasn't time. She'd never make it through the crowd in time to display herself before they kicked the stool out from under the farmer's big clumsy feet.

Luckily she wasn't just a fantastic beauty, she was also a master of disguise. Nobody had recognized her as royalty in the market when she had first seen the Miser, and that was proof enough of her credentials for her. She cupped her hands around her mouth, and disguising her voice, called out, "Oy! Don't he get a final wish? Only proper like and whatnot!"

The Miser thought for the smallest of moments, and then said, "No."

But Willuna had found allies in the audience. A familiar woman with a familiar young girl called out, "Just one last wish!"

Willuna could see the Miser eyeing the crowd. The idea was finding kindling in amongst the town-folk, catching fire as more of the good people caught up with the idea. It burst into flame when the little girl, the very same one who had nearly drowned, was ushered forward by her mother.

"Pwease," she said, her great big eyes puppyish, her little lower lip pushed out and trembling, "Oh pwease mister, pwease?"

"Awwwwww," went the town-folk.

"Ick," went the Miser.

"How can anyone say no to a face like that?" said the leader of the militia.

The Miser leaned down from the edge of the gallows, making the whole platform rumble and squeak, and stuck his face right up close to the girl. "No," he said. "Nooooooo. No and no and no again. No!" He turned back to the men of the militia. "See? It's easy."

But now there were rumblings in the crowd, glances exchanged between the members of the militia. It wasn't their way to just up and hang somebody lickety-split. And to do so just like that, with no last words, no last meal, no final wish? Well that was just downright rude. And wasn't this scarecrow of a man the very same fellow that was constantly accusing this merchant of having his thumb on the scale, or that shopkeeper of selling him rotten apples but only after he had eaten them all up?

The militia leader had had enough. He turned to the farmer and said, "Right then you, what'll it be?"

"I suppose going free is out of the question?"

The militia leader scratched his head and winced. "I'm afraid so," he said, "we all saw those... those things come scampering right for you. Can't have you spreading evil about like butter over bread."

"Well..."

Willuna called out, "How about leaving these good people with a gift?"

The farmer brightened, as much as a fellow with a noose about his neck can manage such a feat anyway. "Yes, good idea," he said. "I wish for all of us, be they man, woman, dwarf or goblin, to live together in peace and-"

"A different kind of gift, a gift of..."

The farmer frowned and shook his head. "Sorry, I'm not-"

"The gift of muuuuu..." said Willuna, urging him on.

"Nope," said the farmer, still not getting it, "I'm not-"

"Play your fricken' fiddle you idiot!" yelled Willuna, then she clapped a hand over her mouth because that is not at all the way proper young princesses talk.

But at least her harsh language had served its purpose. "Yes!" said the farmer. "Absolutely, yes!"

"Absolutely no!" cried the Miser. But he was ignored. As the Miser scurried around the gallows, flapping his hands at the militia and at the crowd the farmer's hands were untied and his bow and fiddle were placed in his hands. The Miser finally cornered the militia leader on the corner of the gallows' platform and insisted on having a word.

But the farmer told him, "No more words," and began to play.

Right feet kicked high, left feet shuffled around. Arms were flung up and heads began to bob. Everyone, everywhere in sight danced like it was the celebration all over again. Town-folk laughed, the Miser screeched, and the leader of the militia said, "Quite good, isn't he?"

And while they danced and jumped and jigged Willuna ran up on the gallows and slipped the noose from around the farmer's neck. She picked up his bow and arrow and together, laughing, they hurried from the town, the farmer playing them all the way out.

This was how Princess Willuna learned that she cared (a begrudging, teeny tiny bit) about whether the farmer, stupid nuisance that he was, lived or died.

***

The moon laced the little tufts of grass clinging to the mountainsides, as if to give them armour against the dark and angry waves of fury that lapped invisibly out from the castle. Big dark clouds hung across the sky, bloated and the colour of corpses. There were no sounds, nothing dared. Even the wind refrained from whistling its way through the sharp mountain tops and valleys.

Inside the castle, in its deepest darkest parts, Bodolomous' laboratory was alive with beakers bubbling, smoke rolling in sickly green furls, and jesters scurrying scurrying scurrying. They'd been sent out further, cast their dead nets wider, emptied a dozen graveyards and then gone back out for more.

In the middle of it all, in a large space cleared on the floor, Bodolomous kneeled, sewing threads as thick as a child's wrist. With each stitch his hate boiled a little hotter, cooking away the man who had just wanted some applause, leaving behind a monster who wanted everything else.

"No more finery!" he shouted, and the jesters wavered in his fury, "No more finesse! Bring me more bodies, bring me them all!"

He'd been treating this like a game. But a game was something that *anybody* could win. A game was something a nothing, nobody farmer could win.

Bodolomous wanted something that only *he* could win. Something where he could ensure that the odds were in his favour. He wanted the whole world to see *his* fist raised in victory at the end. Bodolomous wanted a war.

As the jesters leapt away to do their master's bidding he cried out after them, "And find me the farmer!"

This was how Bodolomous came to realize he had never before truly known the meaning of the word *hate*.

CHAPTER 15

The village was a thing of beauty; except of course that it wasn't beautiful, it was stupendously plain. The houses and stores and dirt roads and the people, the wonderfully beautifully plain people were all solid and normal and doing nothing more than going about their daily business. The celebration's banner had been taken down from across the street, and the stalls had been whisked away. Idwal the farmer was home.

A happy skip kept threatening to introduce itself into Idwal's step, but he did his level best to keep it out. "Prepare yourself," he said to Willuna, "for good solid food, good solid work, and good solid folk. All of our elders are veterans of your father's army. After the wars they wanted a place of absolute peace..."

The princess shuffled on, looking at her feet and not really taking in anything of what was around her. She'd been happy for a bit after rescuing him, but she'd quickly returned to her depression as they'd gotten further away from Owltown. Idwal supposed he could understand; she'd had her heart set on King Anisim her whole life, but that life had been stripped away. He didn't know exactly what had happened between her and the wizard in that room in the inn, but he felt a warm glow whenever he imagined being given the chance to give the magician an even more thorough thrashing. Idwal had to admit he was bothered by her sadness... even if she was something of a spoiled vain twit.

"I'm sorry I couldn't catch the magician for you," he said.

The princess looked up and gave him a small, albeit sad, smile. It raised Idwal's heart a little. "At least you had the courage to try," she replied.

And then Gretal was there, rushing at him, and Idwal almost forgot about the princess. Almost. He opened his arms for a welcoming hug, but Gretal stopped short and took his face in her hands. She turned his head this way, then that, peering up with shrewd examining eyes. "You've changed," she said.

"Oh, not really. It's so good to see you again. You were always in my thoughts, even in my darkest-"

"Is that poetry?" Gretal frowned. "That sounds suspiciously like poetry."

"Poetry? Me? Of course not. I hope that you've been able to go ahead with our wedding plans."

"I have," said Gretal, finally satisfied with her examination.

"I knew I could count on you."

The blessed normality of the moment was broken as a clump of merchants, who clearly should have been at work at that particular point in the day, hurried past. They were followed by another group, store merchants, who had their heads together, muttering.

"What's going on?"

"One of my plans," said Gretal. "Soon you'll be all settled and you'll never fear another adventure again. It's good to have you back." She gave him a smile and then was off, following the crowds.

Idwal turned back to the princess, blushing from the public display of affection. Gretal was no kissing-booth Becky, but that bit about holding his face in her hands had felt rather intimate.

"That can't be your fiancée," said the princess.

"Why not?" said Idwal. "Are you forbidding me? I mean, I know you're the, " he looked around, leaned in close to whisper, "the queen now and all, but I really don't think you're allowed to forbid-"

"I'm not forbidding. I'm telling you as your... your friend."

"I don't understand."

"You don't love her."

"I don't... I'm sorry, but what? I mean, she's..."

"She's what?"

"She's the maiden of my heart's desire. She's plain-spoken and solid and secure and..."

"It sounds like you're describing a house. Where's the love? Where's the affection? Listen to me farmer, Idwal, I know a thing or two about love."

"Here we go with Anisim again!"

"Yes, that's right, and that's King Anisim to you. I'm a princess, and I was raised to be married. Marriage is all I am. And when I think of Anisim I think of his cool head, his dedication, his discipline-"

"Now who's forgetting love? You weren't describing a husband, you were describing a horse."

"You're not in love with Gretal, you just want the girl who most resembles this village of yours."

"How dare... If you weren't my queen-"

"Oh go ahead, say it!"

"*I'm* not in love? *You're* not in love. You don't want to be a wife, you want to be a queen!"

"Oh really?"

"Yes! Really!"

"Well lucky me, I guess I got what I wanted after all! And I only had to have my daddy killed to get it! I wonder why I ever waited so long!"

Idwal's anger dropped away. He blinked, then looked around to see if anyone had been watching. A pair of farmers and their families walked by, but they didn't seem to have heard the argument. They gave Willuna's odd dress a glance, then hurried off down the street in the direction everyone else had gone. "I'm sorry," he said, "I wasn't thinking. Really-"

Another family passed, all heads turning to appraise the princess.

"What is everyone looking at?" she said.

"Come on." Idwal took her hand and led her into one of the shops nearby.

"What is this?" asked the princess, looking around.

"What is... It's a dress shop. How could you, of all people, not know what a dress shop is?"

The princess looked around at the dresses on wooden forms, the rolls of fabric. "But why do you need a store? People come and make them for you, everyone knows that."

"Just... just look around. Find something plain."

As the princess looked around it was clear on her face that she didn't expect to find anything else. She gravitated, naturally, toward the fanciest of the gowns, which while plain to her was what passed for an extravagant wedding gown in the village. "No," said Idwal.

So of course the princess' finely tuned senses instantly directed her to the second most extrava-

"No," said Idwal again.

The princess stomped her little foot, getting really quite frustrated. Idwal snatched up the nearest, simplest dress he could find, a modest and satisfactorally plain thing made of a pale pink fabric, completely devoid of any and all decorations. He shoved it into the princess' arms and, taking her by the shoulders, steered her into the dressing room that stood in the back of the shop.

The princess protested the whole way, it was too plain, it was beneath her, she was pretty sure it wasn't even finished - where was the lacework? The scrolling stitchery? Had she ever mentioned how much she hated him?

Idwal shut the door in her face. He turned, wiped at his face, and found the dressmaker seated on her stool, smiling up at him.

"Ah," said the dressmaker, "young love".

"Ha!" said Idwal, and gave the door a kick. He could almost feel the princess sticking out her tongue in return. He paced, wandering the floor, seeing nothing. Young love? Ridiculous. He did his best to ignore the dressmaker's knowing smile as he shuffled. Nobody could love that spoiled, wilful, ignorant brat. Yes, okay, she'd had a rough time of it. And it was true, fine, that she had probably saved his life from that mob. But still, the dressmaker was miles off, he was engaged to the maiden of his dreams, Gretal, the best girl in the village, and that was that. Story over. End of debate. Right?

There was a flicker off to his left. He turned, looking, not very interested, but happy to be distracted from his thoughts. There was nothing over there but a standing mirror. He walked to it, gave the polished metal a tap. He looked back over his shoulder to see what might have caused the reflection. Behind him dresses stood on stands, pale green, grey, beige... but he could have sworn the movement had been of something black.

Another swirl of black from the next mirror over, smaller, standing on a table. He moved to it, looked in. Nothing.

And again, a twist of blackness, this time from a hand-mirror lying on a stool. He looked over to the dressmaker sewing away in the corner, she had apparently seen nothing (except young love where it clearly was not).

There it was again. Idwal crept up to the hand-mirror, careful as a mouse in a house full of cats. He peered down, and saw the wizard looking right back up at him.

Idwal looked up in the direction of the dressing room. The wizard looked up in the direction of the dressing room. They looked back at each other. Idwal raced to the back of the shop, the wizard sprinting from mirror to mirror beside him. Idwal snatched up a bolt of cloth and rushed into the dressing room, stretching the cloth in front of him to hide the princess.

"You're always trying to see me naked!" She pounded on his chest through the cloth.

Idwal looked back over his shoulder. There was a small mirror hanging on the wall of the dressing room. The wizard glared out from it, looking really very angry. He ran a thumb across his throat and pointed it at Idwal - a promise of death for when they next met. The wizard stepped backwards and vanished, the mirror becoming just a mirror once again.

The dressmaker poked her head into the room. "Alright in here?" she asked.

"Fine," said Idwal.

"It's just I don't go for the shenanigans in here, this is a proper establishment."

"There was a, um, bug, that's all. She hates bugs."

"Ah, a knight in shining armour to the rescue of his lady love eh? Carry on." Before Idwal could object the dressmaker had retreated.

"Are you decent?" Idwal asked over his shoulder.

"Yes," said the princess.

He turned and got a slap right across his face.

"Anisim is going to kill you."

"I'm afraid there's a bit of a line forming for that."

The princess shoved him aside. She looked at herself in the mirror, turned this way, then that. "I look... plain!" she wailed.

Not that he would ever admit it, but Idwal didn't quite agree. In fact, if pressed on the matter, he'd have to say that he thought she looked quite charming. Without all the foofaraw and decorations that she usually carried around, there was only the princess left in that simple dress, and that was more than enough.

He caught himself looking at her in the mirror. And by her expression he knew that she had noticed him noticing her too. Embarrassed and blushing, all this looking back and forth in the mirror was still a far sight better than what had been in the glass moments before.

Idwal gently moved the princess aside and stepped closer to the polished metal. His own face looked back at him. "The wizard," he said. "I know how he gets around."

This was how Idwal realized that even though he found the princess to be quite possibly the most annoying creature in all the human kingdoms, he seemed to always be rushing to her aid.

Not that he would ever admit it.

***

The farmer had bought Willuna the dress using some of the coins her father had given him. That was nice of him, she supposed, though she would have much preferred one of those other fancier options. So he had bought her a dress, which was nice, but had only done it because her old dress was too "conspicuous", whatever that meant, and that wasn't very nice. And then he had just come barging in while she was getting changed, which wasn't nice at all; unless the magician really had been in the mirrors like the farmer said, which meant that the farmer had done something really nice by trying to protect her again.

This was all getting pretty confusing. And not at all the way things were supposed to go. Knights were supposed to protect her, and lords, and kings, not peasants. So why did she feel all warm inside at the thought that this stupid country boy was willing to stand between her and danger?

She was thankful for the distraction of the crowds outside. Their obvious common interest in something unknown let her tip out her wondering about the farmer and refill herself with curiosity about the gathering. The farmer flagged down a passer-by and was told that there was going to be a fire.

"What's that mean?" asked Willuna, but the farmer didn't know. So they followed.

And rounding a corner into the village square stopped dead in their tracks.

"Oh no," said the farmer, and *oh no* was quite right.

Gretal stood in the centre of the square, next to a sawed-off tree stump. Next to her stood a pole with kindling all around it. On the far side of the stump a woman was kneeling, a burlap sack over her head. And standing on the stump itself, shaking his fist at the sky, was the Miser.

"Again?" said Willuna.

"Already?" said the farmer. "What's he doing here?"

"I come to offer the cleansing fire of justice!" cried the Miser. "The plague of deviltry that has sickened the lands of late has come even unto here my friends. Behold the face of evil!"

With that the Miser whisked away the burlap bag, revealing the face of the Old Woman.

***

"'But'?" said the farmer. "What do you mean 'but'? That dear lady out there was there for us when we reached our lowest-"

"Someone has to tell Anisim about the mirrors!"

The farmer had wanted to run right up to the stump and tear the binding ropes away from the Old Woman. But his fellow town-folk were growling, licking their chops. The evils of Owltown hadn't yet reached them here, but they had heard the terrifying tales, and they wanted to cut off the troubles before they got a foothold here at home. The farmer had then reached for his fiddle, but Willuna had asked him if he was willing to turn his back on his home for all time - a place that lived and breathed what was normal and ordinary certainly would never let him stay after he made them all magically dance.

She pulled him into the common room of the most boring inn she had ever seen. They had it to themselves, everyone was out listening to the Miser as he ranted on.

"That fits rather nicely into a letter," said the farmer. "'Dearest Lovebunny…'"

"That's 'King Lovebunny' to you."

"'I like mirrors as much as the next person, actually probably more than the next person, all right I adore mirrors, they're my very favourite past-time but-"

Gretal slipped in, closing the front door behind her. "Here you are," she said. "I didn't get the chance to meet your friend."

"My friend?" said the farmer. "Oh, her. Gretal, this is Wil… er, Wilhemina."

"A pleasure," said Gretal, not sounding very much like she meant it.

"Entirely mine," said Willuna, sounding equally sincere. Willuna had the feeling that she didn't much care for this young woman, though she couldn't say exactly why.

"What did he save you from?"

"I'm sorry?" replied Willuna.

"He was on an adventure, wasn't he? Playing the part of the hero?" Gretal eyed Willuna up and down. "Although the brochures made it seem like the damsel in distress would have much more heave in her-"

"What's going on out there?" said the farmer. "I promised Wilhemina peace and quiet."

"She'll have it soon enough," said Gretal, "once we've done away with that troublemaker."

Willuna looked down at her bosom. "I have plenty of heave," she muttered to herself.

"'We?'" said the farmer to Gretal. "You're in league with the Miser, that shrivelled old grouch? Do you know what he did to me? To us? I can't believe you're responsible for all that!" The farmer thrust a finger out indicating the crowd outside, the stump, and what was sure to be a firey end for the Old Woman.

"I'm not!" said Gretal. "*She* is! Your precious Old Woman!"

Willuna bounced up and down on the balls of her feet, still admiring the upper front part of her dress. "Pert and perky," she said.

Gretal took the farmer's hands in her own. "We have every reason to believe she's behind all the recent troubles. All those graveyards robbed, the evil that befell our good king. Before she came, nothing ever happened. Wonderful, perfect nothing. You should have seen all the strange things she was carrying..." Gretal scratched at her head. "How she managed to keep all that stuff up under her skirts we'll never know. Anyway, none of it could be to our benefit." She looked up into the farmer's eyes. "She's the one who sent you away from me."

"Oh," said the farmer, relenting just a little, "we don't know that for sure."

Gretal stepped back and opened the front door. The Miser was mid-rant, a large collection of odd bits of this and that surrounding his stump, all of it supposedly having been pulled from under the Old Woman's skirts. He thrust a packet of something out over the crowd and shouted, "...and these magic turnip seeds!"

Gretal closed the door.

"Oh," said Idwal, "Well..."

"If you want to be with me," Gretal told the farmer, "this is the only way. You'll see. We'll be back to normal in no time."

Out she went. The farmer went to close the door behind her, staring out at the crowd in disbelief. "They're going to do it," he said. "They're really going to do it."

"Will you stop them?" asked Willuna. "Will you fight them? Will you make them dance if needs be?"

"They're all I've ever known," he said, turning to her.

"No," said Willuna, "they're not. You've known a king who loved your gift, and another king who gave you his trust. You've known seven dwarves who mourned for their lady and you've known a princess who..."

"Who was sad to finally become a queen?"

"Yes. This village is what you know best, but it's not all you know. Will you give up what you know best in order to save the life of an old woman?"

The farmer turned back to look out at the crowd and, Willuna supposed, at Gretal. He looked so very sad and she was surprised to find that she wanted to give him a hug. "Well," he said finally, "I suppose you've had to hide from an entire kingdom." He turned back and gave her a smile that wasn't much of a smile at all. "I suppose it's no very big thing for me to give up a plain old village."

'Well," said Willuna, becoming very imperial, "maybe it won't come to that. Now here is what you're going to do."

"Me?"

"You. They're your people. Don't worry, you'll be adequate."

"I'll be stuttering."

"Nonsense. Stand tall! Chin up! Chest out! Give them poise, show them pageantry!"

"How do I look?"

"Commanding. Righteous. They won't recognize you."

***

The Miser was of course blabbering on, and Idwal wondered how the old crank hadn't yet managed to die from the poison he was spewing out. Apparently the Old Woman was the source of every evil on the planet, from sore feet right through to wars and plagues, and it was the village's job, nay, duty, to put a righteous end to her.

Idwal moved through the crowd, heading for the front, his left foot heavy, his right foot heavier, the both of them seeming to take on the density of lead. There were four rough rows of his fellow villagers left, then three, and every step he took closer to the front of the mob was another silent good-bye.

He could see Gretal up there, standing beside the Miser, looking pretty in spite of herself, and looking fierce. And then there were no more villagers to hide him and he was saying good-bye good-bye good-bye to the maiden of his heart's desire, because there was no hope in him that she'd want anything to do with him after this was all said and done.

Gretal met his eyes and she could read his intent. She looked at him sadly but said nothing to give him any relief.

Idwal gathered in a breath, held it behind his teeth for this one last moment where he still belonged in this silly old village where he'd been born and raised by each and every one of those people around him. And then he let it out like a sword thrust and said, "Did you bring your dancing shoes?" and the Miser shut right up.

Idwal turned to the crowd. "Some of us are too young to remember the wars, thank goodness."

"Well put," said Jan, from the front of the crowd.

"But you elders," Idwal went on, "you were witness to travesties and injustices. I, um, well, I can't help thinking that it must have looked a bit like what's going on here today."

"Oh, quite moving," said the Miser, not so much rolling his eyes as rolling his voice. "She's a witch, she's evil, someone give me a torch."

"Is your case so weak that you wouldn't even let her have a trial?"

"What more proof do you need?" The Miser pointed at the Old Woman who had yet to say a word. "This creature is a consort of devils, a purveyor of malicious potions, a... a... well, I'm forgetting one. Did I show you the evil turnip seeds?"

"You know," said Jan, folding his arms. "The boy has a point. Not much there that really sounds like proof. Now I don't much like the idea of a witch coming round our part of the world, but I like even less the idea that we're the type of folk who'd set a woman on fire just because some stranger said so."

There were murmurs and nods and general all-round assenting in the crowd. Idwal could feel the tide shift. He had done it, just like that, he had saved the Old Woman's life.

The Miser could taste the change in the air too. "Fine," he said, "a trial it is. Where's your nearest river?"

"River?" said Idwal. "What do you need a river for?"

***

They'd retreated back to the inn, Idwal and the princess and the old woman. Idwal had escorted them into one of the rooms. He paced. The princess paced. The old woman sat on the bed, head turning, watching the argument.

"That's the way it's done," said the princess. "Everyone knows that."

"*I* didn't know it," said Idwal. "Just so I'm clear on this... if we see her float-"

"She's a witch."

"Who comes up with these things?"

"It's tradition."

"So is marrying off daughters. So in order to prove her innocence we have to drown her?"

"Precisely."

"Sounds about right," said the old woman, who seemed to be enjoying herself a great deal more than any decent condemned person should.

"But we know she's a witch, what with the wishes..." Idwal glared at the old woman, "the seeds."

"Well," replied the princess, "there's no separate test for good witches and bad witches, so we'll just have to hope we have the right kind. Our real problem is that she's all skin and bones. I've seen ducks with a better chance of drowning."

"Ah!" said Idwal, reaching into his pockets, "I have that covered." He pulled out an assortment of rocks and laid them on the bed. "Your innocence," he told the Old Woman. "They'll weigh you down."

"What if they check her pockets?" asked the princess.

"Ha!" Idwal next pulled out a needle and a spool of thread. "We'll sew them into the hem of her skirts."

"Not bad," said the princess. She grabbed the needle and thread and kneeled at the Old Woman's feet. "Now there's just the little problem of the dear lady's need to breathe."

"There are reeds near the bridge."

"Reeds?"

"They're hollow. Cut one off and you can breathe through it. All the children do it."

"I was a child. I never did it."

"Come to think of it, what do child princesses do?"

"Mainly I was just praised and adored." By this point it had become painfully clear that the princess had absolutely no idea about how one goes about sewing. She held up the needle and thread. "Make this go," she said.

Idwal bent down to take over the sewing duties. There was a knock at the door.

"It's time," said the Miser from the other side.

The princess rushed over to the door. "Just a moment!" she said. She turned back to Idwal and whispered, "There's no lock!"

"We've never needed them," Idwal whispered back.

The princess rolled her eyes. "What is wrong with you people?"

The door handle turned. The princess shoved her shoulder against it. Idwal sewed and sewed. One rock sewn in. Two.

"Let us in!" cried the Miser. "There's justice to be served!"

"I'm not decent!" said the princess.

"Why start now?" asked the Miser, still clawing at the door from the other side.

"Oh now," said Jan's voice from the hallway, "there's no need to get nasty."

Another rock finished. Idwal started on the fourth.

"They're up to something!" yelled the Miser. "In! In! We must get in!"

The door was rammed. The princess tumbled backwards over the bed, knocking the Old Woman off and onto Idwal who landed flat on his back. The Old Woman ended up on top of him in a unfortunately suggestive pose.

"Aha!" shouted the Miser, thrusting out an accusing finger. "I knew I had forgot one! Succubus!"

***

The crowd moved, sluggish and dull, down to the river. The Miser had his yellowed twiggish fingers dug into the Old Woman's arm, dragging her along. Idwal fought his way through, trying to protest. He saw the princess ahead of him, jogging alongside the Miser. He could hear her, saying how the king would never allow such a travesty as this trial to go on, that he had always been a friend to magic-users.

The Miser was one of those people who had the amazing ability to completely not hear whatever they didn't wish to take in. So it was with the princess' protests; she might as well have been yelling into a hole in the ground for all the impact she made.

They made the edge of the river. Idwal shouldered his way through the crowd. "This drowning deal is ridiculous!" he said. "Couldn't we just ask her a lot of strongly-worded questions? Like 'hey are you evil you gosh-darned old, um, hag?'"

The Miser turned to him, smiled. "No more words." He turned to address the crowd. "And now we shall see! In the name of the king, let this trial commence!"

"Wait!" said Idwal. "If she's so all-powerful why haven't we all been turned into toads or bats or some other thing that little boys put into the pockets of little girls?"

"Hm," said Jan, rubbing a hand over his bald head. "The boy has a point. A very good point."

"A splendid point indeed," said the Miser, all courtesy, and then he shoved the Old Woman into the water. "Oops."

The Old Woman made very little splash, and bobbed up almost instantly. Her many skirts swirled around her as the water pushed her along. Idwal threw off his vest and kicked off his boots, readying himself to jump in after her.

"Why not give her a moment?" said the Miser, in a reasonable tone of voice which irritated Idwal right down to the roots of his hair. "Let us all see her innocence and be done with it. You *are* sure she's innocent, aren't you?"

Idwal ground his teeth. He had no idea what to do - save the old woman but let the accusation of witch-craft lead her right to a fiery ending or let her go under and prove her innocence. He looked around desperately for the princess, wanting her advice, but she'd vanished. Idwal felt let down, he had just been coming to count on her... mainly for insults, but still it would have been good to have someone from outside his village's mind to give him perspective.

"My my," said the Miser, strolling along like it was a lazy Sunday afternoon, "look at her float."

"Sink woman, sink," muttered Idwal under his breath.

"And she's floating, and she's floating..." The Miser rubbed his hands together. "So, who has a tinderbox? Or we could just stone her to death from here, I'm flexible."

And then the Old Woman went under.

"Yes!" shouted Idwal, "look at that old bag drown!" He turned to the Miser. "I think a celebration is in order. Care to join? I'm a mean hand on the old fiddle."

Much to Idwal's surprise there wasn't anything to be seen on the Miser's face. For a cranky old fellow who spent most of his time broad-casting his various displeasures to the world he seemed rather sedate. Idwal felt like he'd been robbed. He knew it wasn't very nice of him but he really wanted to get a good gloating in. But instead of being a good sport the Miser merely shrugged his pokey shoulders, then turned and began to walk off.

Idwal hurried around to block the old boy off. "That's it?" Idwal said. "You're just going to toddle off after all that talk about justice?"

Idwal looked down. The Miser had a small heavy bag in his hands. It jingled a little as the Miser withdrew his fingers and pulled tight its drawstrings. "I'm fine either way. Now, out of my way boy, I have some serious counting to do."

Idwal let the Miser brush by. Someone had paid the old crow of a man. This hadn't been about justice, at least as far as the Miser was concerned, it had only been a show. Who would do such a thing? The magician was the only person Idwal could think of who would do something so rotten, but what good would it do him? Did the magician hate the Old Woman? Was this a distraction? If so, a distraction from what?

Idwal's head snapped around.

Where was the princess?

But what about the Old Woman? She couldn't still be alive down there, could she? What chance a witch could conjure herself a set of gills?

He didn't know if the princess needed his help. He didn't know if the Old Woman was past needing his help. He stood still, desperate to go dashing off in two directions at once.

But in the end, he at least knew where the Old Woman was, more or less. He would have to leave the princess' whereabouts a mystery for now, even though the not knowing made for a dull aching place in his chest. Idwal pushed past the villagers and waded out into the river, finally diving under where the river bottom made a sudden steep downturn.

He swam down, scanning, moving through the orange-brown light that the river let shine through. A couple of bossy-looking trout swam along, giving him a quick inspection as they flashed by.

He turned to look upstream, then turned again and looked the other way. He stopped, and broke out in a grin. The Old Woman was there, halfway between the surface and the bottom, breathing through a reed. Below her, hanging onto the Old Woman's ankle with one hand and a rock with the other was the princess. She also had a reed clenched in her fingers, but it was obvious that the surface was far too distant for the reed to reach. As Idwal swam toward them the princess smiled up at him, waved hello with a finger, then her eyes closed and she drifted away.

CHAPTER 16

Off in the Castle Wolf Anisim was pacing, pacing. Reports skittered across the table with every pass he made like drifts of snow. No good news, no hope to be found in all of that ink.

"More raids," he said, consulting only himself, "more robberies, and the mystery goes on and on. What are you up to magician? And do I really want to find out?"

There was really no question though, he didn't have a choice. He had to find out what evil the magician was cooking up, that's what a king did. He wondered what the farmer was up to at that moment. Was he back to growing his vegetables? Did he have Willuna hoeing dirt? He could just picture the look on her face. He cracked a smile, the first in days.

He sighed and turned to a tapestry hanging on the wall. It was a battle scene, a depiction of his father leading a charge against an unidentified foe (though the leader of the opposition bore a striking resemblance to King Torquil). Anisim had always had the feeling that his father had preferred the war years, back when the enemy was the enemy and that was that. In peace times there just wasn't anything for a warrior to hit. So the late king had taken all of that warrior energy and zeal and focused it on his son who could never quite please his father.

"I admit it, old man," Anisim said, squinting at the threads that made up his father's face, "I am lost, confused, bumbling around in the dark. You win again. Everything you said you saw in me is true. Something's coming and I don't know what, or where it's going to hit."

A knock at the door.

"Enter."

A guard came in, delivered a letter.

"Ah good," said the young king, "I was worried I was running out of bad news."

Anisim dismissed the guard. He was going to toss the letter on top of the rest of the ill tidings but then noticed the seal. There was no official seal, but someone had swirled the rough outline of a round vegetable into the red wax. And in just the right light, that round vegetable could very well be taken for a turnip.

Anisim snapped the letter back up and cracked open the seal. He flipped open the letter and found Willuna's handwriting within. After a great long and extremely flowery greeting she got to the meat of it - the farmer had figured out how the magician was moving around so quickly, how he kept slipping out of the grasp of justice in all of the kingdoms, how he was making just a great big nuisance of himself.

"Good work farmer," Anisim said, then threw open his door to call to his guard. "Assemble everyone! *Every*one!"

This was how King Anisim learned how the magician was moving around so quickly and making a great big nuisance of himself. I would have thought that was quite obvious, really.

***

Breathe! thought Idwal.

Live!

He'd motioned the Old Woman up out of the water, and caught up with the princess and carried her limp form out of the river. Now the princess lay on the bank, less life in her than a landed trout.

The crowd was close around, a murmuring half-circle of long faces. There wasn't any hope in them, and they didn't have any help to offer.

But Idwal had seen this before, this very same thing. A girl on a riverbank, waiting for someone to give her permission to continue on with her life. But there was no King Anisim this time with his magic kiss, the princess would have to make do with a frightened farmer who was feeling completely helpless.

Idwal picked up her hand and gave it a brisk rubbing. Nothing. He poked her in the ribs. Gave her long hair a tug. If nothing else he figured he could annoy her back up on to her feet. But the princess did nothing, not a gasp or a flutter. A frightening blue was starting to creep in around her lips.

There was nothing else for it. Idwal leaned over and joined his lips with hers. A new round of muttering broke out of the crowd; the boy was gathering a growing list of dailiances with strange women - first the Old Woman, now a dead girl. Someone should really take him aside for a good long talk.

Idwal stayed like that, mouth pressed down to the princesses, blushing for a number of reasons. His eyes looked around, there was still no reaction from the princess. What could he have expected? Magic kisses obviously lay within the domain of kings… he was overstepping his bounds again.

Idwal sighed. Right into the princess' mouth.

And she coughed up a lung's worth of water in his face.

The crowd shifted back, uneasy. "Zombie!" shouted a boy, pointing. "He's made a zombie!"

Idwal didn't need to look back, he could feel his fellow villagers slipping even further away from him. First the strange woman, then the turnip, then this new strange woman, and now he was making seemingly dead girls cough. He was no longer plain, and far from ordinary.

And as he helped the princess sit up Idwal found that he no longer truly cared.

***

Wolf soldiers stomped down grey halls, barging into every room. Everywhere they charged the sound of shattering glass soon followed. Soon there wasn't a single mirror left in all of Castle Wolf.

And then they went further, the knights mounting and galloping from the castle, taking the news of Idwal's discovery to every human home in every human kingdom. In another day or two they could rest safe, the magician would be trapped on the far side of wherever the mirrors led.

People began to breathe a little easier, to feel a little safer. They thought the worst of it was over.

The people were wrong.

CHAPTER 17

The inn in the village, the Pale Pony, had never been livelier. And all because of the alive-again girl with the long lovely hair. Willuna sat, looking lovelier than she ever had before in the light of the healthy wood fire, and not knowing a bit of it. Not caring either. There was food to eat. Fantastic food. Wonderful food. The finest she'd ever eaten.

She shovelled stew and chomped bread. Tasted wine and let it dance around her mouth. The farmer sat across from her, collecting as many sideways glances as she was, and caring just about as much.

"I think maybe the magician paid the Miser to prosecute the Old Woman. I thought it was to distract me so he could get at you... you're sure you didn't see him at all?"

"Nmmm..." Willuna shovelled more food into her mouth.

"Then what..." The farmer took a sip of his ale and wiped at his lips. "It's all connected somehow, I'm sure of it. I just can't put it together."

"Are you done with that?" Without waiting for an answer Willuna lunged across the table and snatched the last bit of bread from the farmer's plate and used it to wipe out her bowl. As she nommed and chewed she realized the farmer was staring at her with a grin. "Never been so hungry," she said and downed the last of the wine. The farmer continued to stare at her. "What?"

"You saved her," said the farmer.

Willuna stopped chewing. She dipped her head. She suddenly found it hard to look him in the eyes. His gaze felt heavy, but exceedingly pleasant. The way he was looking at her, he'd never done it quite that way before. Willuna then understood what she was seeing... admiration. "Well," she said, and for the very first time in her life she felt shy, "one of my subjects was in peril."

"And a queen could do no less."

They looked at each other across the table.

"You know," said the farmer, "I think you're going to fit in that throne just fine." He leaned in. "I feel an overwhelming urge to bow to you right now. But since you're supposed to be in disguise, I hope you'll just take my word on it when I say that I'm very glad that you're my queen."

She didn't feel very queenish at the moment. She felt warm. Like a schoolgirl who had just passed an important test. Like a girl at her very first dance. Like a woman...

She reached out a hand and flagged down Gretal. She held out her bowl. "May I have another please?"

"You liked it?" Gretal fixed Willuna with her usual disapproving glare.

"I've never tasted better. What is it?"

"Turnip stew."

Willuna burst out laughing.

***

The night was unusual in that it was quiet. Very, very quiet. Willuna passed it in the inn while the farmer went off to see what the days away had made of his home. The nearly complete lack of sound reminded Willuna of being under the river. Back home at the castle there would have always been the little noises - the distant footfalls of sentries making their rounds, servants working up the last of their daily duties. Here in this village with no name there was nothing - no drunkards wandering the streets, even the local dogs seemed to have agreed to keep it down.

This quiet, more than anything else, made her understand that this was the furthest she had ever been from home, despite the fact that the castle lay only a good day's walk away. She didn't think she'd be able to sleep, despite the fact that being drowned really did take it out of a body. As it turned out she slept like a log.

She awoke to the good sounds of villagers greeting each other, a cock calling out the daybreak, and proper warm sunlight bursting into her room. She leapt from the bed.

She dressed happy-quick. She went down and ate and then gathered up an extra breakfast, sending smile after smile Gretal's scowling way. For just this little breath of time in this silly little village she felt like she could throw off her tiaras, her curtsies and her bows, and just be a girl. She knew it couldn't last, that there was a crown waiting for her, but that just made this moment all the sweeter.

She bounced back upstairs, carrying the morning sun in her as only a healthy and happy young woman can do, and rapped at the Old Woman's door. In she went. "I've brought you breakfast," she said, setting the tray on the small table beside the bed. "Turnip pancakes, if you can believe it. I know these people want to be plain, but really, there's more than one dullish vegetable in the world." She skipped over to the window and flung open the shutters. "Aren't they silly? Silly but kind." She turned to the Old Woman who was propping herself up in the bed. "And how are you?"

"Breathing," said the Old Woman with a smile, "thanks to you. Would you get the door dearie?" The Old Woman drowned her pancakes with syrup. "Lock it too, if you please. Don't want any old body interrupting our girl talk. That's a lamb." She dug in, chewing with a gusto that belied her rickety frame. Her appetite seemed more appropriate for a woman half her age and carrying twice the meat on her bones.

"I have to say that when I first laid eyes on you I saw nothing but a spoiled brat."

"Yes… well," said Willuna, seating herself on the chair near the bed. She sounded just like the farmer. She tucked a lock of hair behind her ear and stared down at her hands, embarrassed.

"But you," said the Old Woman, pointing at the princess with a dripping knife, "you surprised me. There! Admitted! You were willing to sacrifice yourself for me and sacrifice is a very serious thing. I should know, I gave and I gave… It's a bit of a pity really. You could have made a decent queen."

"Why, thank you," said Willuna, beaming. This really was turning out to be a grand old day. But then her mind skipped a bit, and her smile froze on her face. "Wait," she said, "how did you know who I am?"

And then there was a bad bit of silence. The question hung between them thick as the syrup on the Old Woman's pancakes.

"Oops," said the Old Woman finally, setting aside the breakfast tray. "Is my face red?"

***

If you asked Gretal if this story was about her, she'd tell you that nothing good ever came from being in a story. Certainly there were all those tales with happy endings, but they were all trickery and lies. Because that one little happy ending wasn't really the ending, it was just a pause in time where you decided to stop because you didn't want to carry on with the tale and hear the rest. And that happy ending held another lie in its heart because it made you forget all of the betrayal and the pain and the terror that came before. No, she'd stay clear of our story if she could, thank you very much. She'd already been in one, and it was already the stuff of legend.

No adventures for Gretal, no sally-forths. She had her village and she had her schedule and she had her man. Well, she was sure of two out of those three anyway. And if the third leg of her security was coming loose, she would just concentrate all that much more on the first two.

So, her schedule. She woke at the same time she did every day. She was downstairs making breakfast for her guests at the same time she always did, and if they weren't down in time that was their too bad. But the strange girl Idwal had brought home was actually down before Gretal, waiting with a smile that Gretal really wanted to take a whack at with her wooden spoon. The girl was wearing the same dress as yesterday, which of course made her all that much odder. Granted, Gretal looked exactly the same every day, but that was because her closet contained multiple copies of the one grey dress. She wore the same look out of choice, not poor personal hygiene.

Breakfast had been doled out. Pots and plates scrubbed and cleaned. Now it was time for laundry - linens, to be specific. She went room to room, collecting bedspreads and towels in a big wicker basket.

She cleaned out the Beige Room, the Grey Room, the Don't Do Anything I Wouldn't Do Honeymoon Suite, then stopped at the next door. It was closed, the room that old witch was staying in, and there were voices murmuring through. She had never bothered listening in on a guest's conversation before, but never before had a guest been responsible for peeling away her fiancée.

So she listened. And she learned.

Everything she feared was true.

The Old Woman talked. She was indeed a witch. A very powerful witch. When she wasn't been sought out for her beauty, she was being wooed by those who wanted a touch of her power.

She had mentored a young wizard, many years ago. His parting gift was to foul her magic mirror, trapping her in the disguise of an old crone that she wore to this day.

From then on... revenge! Hunting, probing, tracking and scouring, sniffing down any little trace of the ungrateful worm who had stolen her beauty. This aged body failing her more and more every day, she had begun to court champions. Knights who lived to service the weak and undeserving. Warriors who lived only for their next great challenge. All had failed to draw out the wizard.

If the mighty failed, what about the meek?

"Idwal," whispered Gretal.

It had worked. Oh so well. The witch's latest buffoon, a nothing from nowhere, had foiled the magician. The witch laughed, her cackle crackling through the door - she would have loved to see the wizard's face when he found he was being bested by a turnip farmer! And now the world was set against the wizard.

"But," Gretal heard the strange girl say, "if someone kills your wizard how will you get your beauty back?"

"You know," said the Old Woman, "when he came to me, that boy with his eyes shining bright at the thought of all he could do, he thought the same as you. He thought that life could never be just one thing. That fire didn't just eat up, but it also spit out logs whole and ready to be burned again. Do you know what wisdom is? It's the knowledge that you can become just one thing. That rivers only flow one way. I've lived years now with one thought. It's not just what I think, it's what I eat morning, noon, night, and for a midnight snack.

The beautiful woman in me is gone, and I don't care. All I want is revenge. All I *need* is revenge. There are no more layers to this here onion dearie."

"What does this have to do with me?"

"Nothing," said the Old Woman. "I thought you were going to end up like your dear old dad."

In the hallway, Gretal gasped. She clapped a hand over her mouth. The king-killer was in her inn. Her safe, secure, plainest-of-the-plain inn.

"You killed my father?" she heard the strange girl say. Except of course the strange girl was no longer just strange. In the space of a sentence she'd been stepped from annoying right on up to royal. A great big step indeed.

"Killed him?" the Old Woman cackled. There was far too much glee in her voice. "That would be far too easy. Oh no, oh no indeed. He's alive in there my girl, peering out of his stone eyes, smelling the rain through his chiselled nose. For now and always. You think the magician could have come up with something so pitiless? So absolutely vile? I don't, not by a good old country mile."

Gretal was a statue herself, standing outside that door. Looking right at its faded wood grain, but seeing absolutely nothing. Despite her very best efforts, another story had found her. And it was just as bad as the first.

"So!" the witch went on, "now what to do about our plucky farmer friend? I set up a great big adventure here to drive him back out of this nothing little bend in the road. He was supposed to play the hero and save me, and in doing so get himself a right old shunning so he could never hide in this hole they call a village ever again. He'd be out in the world, aggravating that worm Bodolomous with his every breath. But you went and ruined that, didn't you? I guess I'll need a new adventure for our knight in corduroy armour. Hmmm... if only I had a damsel in distress."

"He's home," Gretal heard the princess whisper, "where he wants to be. He'll never come after me."

"You blind little fool," said the Old Woman, and in her heart Gretal knew the witch was right.

"I won't let you hurt him," said the princess.

"I don't want to hurt him. I want him to do his job for me."

"You're going to get him killed. I'll warn him."

"I can command lightning. I can order spiders to dance. I've got the feel of a child's strangling throat in my fingertips and words of plagues resting in my skull." The Old Woman laughed. "Not a word, dear girl, not a whisper. Or I'll not only acquaint your young man with living nightmares, but I'll send his whole silly village with him."

Idwal came up the steps, great big springs in his heels. Here was a look that sent Gretal's already-sinking heart spinning right down into the deeps. There was an eagerness there, and Gretal knew it wasn't for her.

"Idwal," she said, holding up a hand.

"Yes?"

Now was the time for her to warn him, to keep him from planting his foot in the trap that was waiting to spring on the other side of the door. But that would put her on the page, printed like all the others, bound by covers, her pain forgotten when all the others had won their victories.

"Nothing," she said, and stepped away.

***

In came the farmer. The farmer with his trusting tanned face. With his shy smile that widened when his eyes met hers.

He was so trusting, this boy from the village that had no name.

"Good morning," he said to them both, taking off his hat. He turned to the Old Woman. "Did you sleep well?"

"Like a princess without a pea."

"Ah," said the farmer, "I'll take that as a yes?" And then he was looking at her. Opening his mouth to ask about her night.

"You should knock," Willuna said, her voice giving out halfway through.

"I'm sorry?" said the farmer, still smiling, not knowing what he was sharing a room with. "I didn't quite catch-"

"I said," said Willuna, drawing herself up, making herself royal, making herself a queen, "that you should knock before entering a lady's room. You've forgotten your place."

The farmer's smile dimmed. It hurt Willuna's heart, watching that. It was like the sun being blocked out by a blizzard... wavering...

"Now that we are out of danger," Willuna continued, "you will address me as 'your Majesty.'"

...and the smile was gone.

"You're royalty?" The Old Woman clapped a surprised hand to her mouth. "I had no idea."

"That is all," said Willuna, and did the hardest thing she had ever done. She turned her back on the farmer and stuck her nose in the air. "You may go."

There was quiet. It was diseased, that silence. Every breath of it hurt Willuna more.

"Have I, um..." the farmer swallowed. "Have I done something wrong?"

"I said that was all." Willuna spun around, shouting. "Get out!"

"Now hold on girl," said the Old Woman.

"Get out get out get out!"

The farmer just stood there, looking dazed. Willuna would have to turn the dagger one more time. "Don't you have some turnips to tend?"

She couldn't have slapped him any harder. The farmer gave the Old Woman a sick little nod, and then turned and made his way out of the room, closing the door behind himself. Willuna sank into the chair. "His face," she said, "did you see his face?"

"Oh I did indeed," said the Old Woman. "I simply had no idea he loved you that much."

Willuna looked up. "What?"

The Old Woman smiled. "I'm a bit jealous. I don't think I've ever managed to be so cruel. My hat's off to you, young miss. If ever this royalty thing doesn't work out, look me up. There's a job in wicked-witching for you." The Old Woman scooted herself off the bed and began to dress. "Still, he'll come. There's no amount of cruelty that would stop him. The magician is as good as mine."

CHAPTER 18

Willuna shuffled through the village. It seemed to her that she didn't have the energy to lift her feet and never would again.

The Old Woman spindled on ahead like an insect crossing water. She turned back, eyes sharp in the loose weathered folds of her face. "Quick-step hup! Double-time girlie, double and double again! Do you want me to go after the farmer myself? Then let's see some snap in your step!"

"What do you want from me?" said Willuna. "How can I call your magician out? We smashed all the mirrors. Ground them to dust."

"Ha!" said the Old Woman, and barrelled on toward the well that sat near the center of the village. "Nothing's ever as simple as it seems."

***

Idwal was at work. He tugged weeds. Fixed a fence. Hoed rows and watered growths. He'd been away too long, yes. Away from home. Away from where he belonged. Ridiculous, him getting mixed up in the business of royals. Foolish, foolish farmer.

Every other bit of work done, he turned to that great big hole in the middle of his neat ordered field. Its edges were still rough and uneven from where he had dragged that mutant turnip up out of the ground.

Well, he couldn't very well expect it to fill itself in. He grabbed up his hoe and sent dirt cascading down. It filled up quickly, and in almost no time at all it was like the turnip had never been there. Now it was just a matter of figuring out what would take its place. Lettuce? Tomatoes? For some reason he didn't feel any great desire to plant something that did the majority of its growing underground, out of sight.

A slim shadow fell across the soil. Gretal was there, watching him turn the earth. "Come to help?" he said.

She took a moment, studying his face. Idwal stood up from his hoeing. "Once upon a time," said Gretal, "a happy little brother and a happy little sister were left in the woods. They found kindness in a smiling crone who gave them shelter in her house made of sweets. But it was all a trick, for the crone was a wicked thing who filed her teeth on the bones of children. They, the children… *we*, we fooled her and shoved her into her own oven. How she howled. How she screamed."

"Brave little boy. Brave little girl."

Gretal turned and looked back down the road toward the heart of the village. "There's always another house of candy." She turned back to Idwal. "I've done something awful."

"You?" said Idwal. "But you never do anything, anything at all. That's why we get along so well. Once we're married-"

"Stop," said Gretal. "Listen."

"What is it?"

"There's always another crone."

***

The Old Woman turned the crank, and from down in the heart of the earth up came a bucket brimming with water. She grabbed the bucket and tipped it over, emptying the water back down the well. It made no sound, the bottom was too far away.

"Come worm," she said to Willuna, "on to your hook."

Willuna peered over the side of the well. She saw nothing but darkness. She looked up at the crone, pleading.

"It's you or the village." The Old Woman gave the bucket a wiggle.

Willuna climbed in. Much to her surprise she didn't plummet down all at once. The Old Woman had strength in her that outmatched the looks of her broomstick arms.

She descended, one slow crank of the well's handle at a time. She wondered if this was Anisim's life as a king, one bucket after another.

She slid out of reach of the sun.

***

There was no *plain* left in Idwal, no more *average*. The beige and grey had been blasted out of him by Gretal's recounting of what she had heard. Idwal was a tornado crashing through the village's marketplace, disapproving looks just got blown aside.

"The girl, you've seen her? This high, yes? Little upturned nose, likes to stick it in the air."

Nothing and more nothing. Nobody had seen Willuna. The tornado blew itself out. But then Idwal heard a familiar voice:

"Rocks!" the voice called out. "We've got rocks!"

Idwal turned the last corner in the marketplace and found a long low stall filled with seven dwarves. A wide variety of rocks sat along their counter-space.

"Oy," said Cosimo the dwarf, "it's you."

"Yes, I'm afraid so," said Idwal. "I need your help. Please. The young woman I was with, have you seen her?"

The dwarves scratched heads, stroked beards. "Can't say as we have," said Dietwald. "Care to purchase a rock? They're fresh."

"What would I do with it?"

"Why, the same thing as everyone else. What an odd question."

"What's wrong with this girl?" asked Cosimo, speaking for the bunch. "You're looking rather frantic."

"I've let her get away. I let myself be tricked. I've done everything wrong, everything. If I'd had even the smallest smidgen of sophistication, just the tiniest little bit, I could have seen that there was something wrong. Instead I acted like just what I am, a hick, a nobody… and now I've left her to face some terrible danger all alone."

"Poor fellow," said Dietweld. "We have just the rock for you!"

The other dwarves shoved Dietwald to the back of the stall.

"Don't give up boy," said Egon, "don't you ever give up."

"What could I possibly do?" Idwal threw his hands up into the air. "I know turnips, not swords and sorcery. What could I possibly do that others couldn't do better? There's no hope."

"No hope?" said Gerhard. "No hope you say? There's always hope. Look!"

The dwarves whisked away the rocks, twirled away the cloth over the counter-top, revealing Snow-Drop in her shining glass casket.

"You see?" cried Udo. "This beloved girl was poisoned not once but three times and yet her heavenly bosom still rises and falls!"

"For yourself!" said Friedemann.

"For all of us!" bellowed Egon.

"Fight!" cried Cosimo.

"Yes!" Idwal pumped his fist in the air, carried by the courage in the voices of the dwarves. Still in his heroic pose, he eyed Snow-Drop in her casket. "Sooo... you're using her as a counter-top?"

Gerhard shrugged. "We needed the table-space."

***

The well held autumn airs in its depths. Willuna shivered as she dropped below the summer sun's reach. She looked back up at the coin of light far above, saw a bite in the circle that was the silhouette of the Old Woman's head. And then the silhouette was gone, darting away out of sight.

The bucket plummeted, then jerked to a stop just above the black water, its sides bruising Willuna's legs. Willuna looked up. The silhouette was back. She thought of calling out that the Old Woman could have killed her, but that seemed ridiculously obvious, and she wasn't really sure that the Old Woman would particularly care. The witch had said she was going to use Willuna as bait for Idwal, who in turn was bait for the magician, but Willuna couldn't see how a princess and a farmer stuck down in a well were going to do the witch's plan much good.

"There once was a girl," she muttered, "who went down a well; she had grand plans but they all went to-"

"Princesssssss..." The wizard's voice, a mocking tone. The whisper echoed around the stone walls of the well.

"Show yourself magician," said Willuna, doing her very best to sound commanding and not at all scared, "I would have words with you."

"Words?" said the voice that seemed to be coming from all sides at once. "It's far too late for words."

"Be wise, be reasonable. There are no more mirrors. You're done." Willuna looked up at that silhouette far overhead. "He's here!" she called up to the witch. "I think. Somewhere. Anyway, come and get him." The silhouetted head tilted this way, then that. And then it was joined by a second head. And a third.

And then they tilted over the edge of the well and began to clamber down, easy as spiders. Willuna's eyes went wide. Jesters!

"Wisely, reasonably," said the wizard's voice, "did you really think it was the mirrors?"

The voice no longer echoed. It now came from only one place, below her. Willuna peered over the bucket, down into the water just below. A fourth jester was there to match the reflections from the three above. But this was no silhouette, it was clear and defined as its arms shot up out of the water and grabbed hold of her shoulders, pulling her down into the water.

And then the well was empty, not a single ripple marring the water's surface.

***

Willuna felt twisted and turned, like a rag being squeezed dry in gentle hands. She was travelling, speeding, and then she just like that she was on a stone floor. She was dizzy, she felt as if her brain was spinning like a carousel inside her skull. She closed her eyes. Felt the cold and damp of the stones beneath her.

Stick-figure hands grabbed her around the arms and hefted her to her feet. She was hauled along lifeless corridors, around spider-webbed corners, and finally dumped in a room that sounded like it went on for ever.

Willuna opened her eyes. And found herself face-to-face with a soldier in rough armour. Rougher still was the soldier himself, what with its being made up of bits and pieces of various dead people. His jawbone had once belonged to the face of a very large man, his cheekbones had once been the possession of someone very skinny. One eye was brown, the other blue with the whites turned to black. A beetle investigated the flat hole of one nostril, and a garden snake played along the ladder of his exposed spine. Also, he smelled really really bad.

Willuna screamed and lunged to her feet. She spun and went to run, but there was another undead soldier right behind her, blocking the way. He was in an even more awful state that the first. More soldiers stepped up around them, blocking her in, tightening her little circle of space. She felt sick at the thought of those dripping hands touching her, running through her hair.

There was no space left. Willuna squeezed shut her eyes and screamed again.

But nothing touched her. She opened one squinting eye and peeked out. Some of the soldiers were stepping aside, making a lane. And from this lane walked Bodolomous, looking disgustingly happy with himself. "Why," he said, sneering, "there's a princess in my castle. Wonders never cease."

CHAPTER 19

Idwal made good time, as people in this tale invariably do. He approached the Castle Wolf, his eyes roaming over the business of ramparts and moat. The pennants above snapped like a driver's whip.

A great deal of language clattered down on his head from above as he approached the moat. The language was saucy, to say the least, and very much not the kind of thing we shall reprint here. Idwal shaded his eyes and looked up.

Up and over to his right, on those walking-parts of the walls where sentries were always doing their rounds, was King Anisim. He was the source of the sailor-like vocabulary. He had a canvas set up on a three-legged easel, and he looked out of place with a painter's pallet balanced on his arm. Apparently the painting hadn't been much to the king's liking since Anisim was stabbing it vigorously with the end of his paintbrush. A guard rushed up to the king and whispered in his ear.

The king turned and looked down over the wall's edge. "Farmer?" he said.

"I've made a terrible mistake."

***

Idwal was escorted in, and up. Through halls, up stairs. It was a stark contrast to the Castle Owl; here there wasn't much decoration, and what few tapestries did hang from the wall all seemed to have war and beheadings and rather severe forms of justice as their subjects.

And then the king was there, smiling, gripping his arm in welcome. His smile dropped as Idwal recounted all that had happened regarding Willuna since they had last been in each other's company.

Anisim poured wine for them both. "Silly, wilfull, stubborn..." The king clenched a fist. "Help me think up other words!"

"Um... cheeky?"

Anisim snorted. "Yes," he said, "that too." He passed a goblet to Idwal.

"To cheeky girls?" said the farmer.

"And the poor men they drag along with them."

And then the king was all business. He summoned a guard, told her to get his knights assembled and mounted in the courtyard as soon as possible.

As soon as possible was a surprisingly short time. Anisim led Idwal down to the courtyard. He stood on the rampart steps and, looking very kingly, addressed his mounted knights below, informing them of the subject of their hunt. "If you find her," he said, "be polite, be reasonable, and when that fails send word for me. Off with you, go hunt our beloved prey."

Idwal felt his chest loosen a little, felt he might be able to breathe again. He realized how tense he'd been since the princess had gone missing. But here was Anisim, being all kingly and giving kingly orders. Idwal wished he could give orders like that. But then again he didn't really have anyone to give orders to; he suspected rutabagas would probably do their best to ignore him. At any rate, Anisim was handling things now, and everything was sure to be alright.

It was right about then that the castle's moat exploded outward with an undead army and Idwal's world turned itself upside-down.

***

"How could you?"

"How couldn't I?"

"This is vile, repulsive..."

"Thank you, thank you."

"And horribly smelly."

The magician stopped in his tracks. "Well, yes," he nodded in concession, "there is that."

All around them the skeletons and cadavers were clinking and clanking, jostling themselves as they made their way to, and through, the dozens of great mirrors that lined the cavernous room.

The wizard was scurrying to and fro, making sure his soldiers were making it through, pulling aside the ones that lost a leg here and there and were gumming up the process.

Willuna chased him, her temper burning out her fear. "You wanted the notice of royalty?" she said. "Well now you have yourself a queen. A good queen, a fair and merciful queen, a queen who will not order you to drink poison."

"That's quite decent of you."

"Or tell you to set yourself on fire."

"Ouch."

"Or cut off your own head and present it to me."

"Well that doesn't even make sense."

"Sense?" shouted Willuna, "you're worried about making sense? You've robbed graves, shanghaied loved-ones, to make your rotten army. How does that make sense?"

"I don't have to feed them," said the wizard, looking entirely pleased with himself, "so that's a coin or two saved. Very economical."

"You'll hurt people. Get them killed. Stop this madness," Willuna said, "stop it now!"

"No."

"Why not?"

"Because," said the wizard with a wicked smile, "I'm winning."

***

Idwal was in a battle. A real honest-and-true fight. He had actual *enemies*, enemies that were coming toward him, and if they got close enough they would hurt him, cut him open, leave him for the birds, and move on to their next victim. He had no training to fall back on, no soldier's instincts. The clash and clang of swords meeting swords rolled over him like breakers on a shore. He couldn't have felt more like floundering if he had been at sea.

They kept coming, these half-fleshed things, rolling up out of the castle's moat. Their smell alone was enough to unnerve him. The putrescence painted the air and clung to the skin, made its way down his throat. The moat circled the castle completely, and the enemy was coming from all sides. Idwal stumbled back, but there really wasn't a "back" to speak of, because they were surrounded. Idwal banged against Wolf soldiers who were running for the main gates, bounced off them and got tangled up with a line of archers making for the tops of the walls. He had no sense of place in this mess, no idea what he should be doing. He didn't know if he could help, or if he should even try. He might just end up interfering, making things worse.

But then there was Anisim, the Wolf King. His voice cut through the clamour. He commanded soldiers to their posts, arranged archers on the walls. The next moment he was at the gate, swinging a great broadsword, smashing his way through the undead. Fighting alongside his soldiers, urging them forward, showing them the way. They moved the enemy at the gates back, step by step, the dismantled undead splashing down off the sides of the drawbridge. Anisim filled them with hope. Hope that they could make it through this horror. Faith that they could wake up from the nightmare.

And then Anisim stopped, dead in his tracks. His arms went limp, he dangled his sword from his side. The Wolf King had stopped fighting.

***

Willuna stood in the middle of the great room, watching the battle through the mirrors arranged around the walls. "How?" she said. "We broke all the mirrors!"

Bodolomous stood next to her, hands behind his back, rocking on his feet. He was beaming, like a proud father watching his young son accomplish something especially manly. "It's not mirrors," he said, in the tone that reminded Willuna of one of her old tutors, "it's the reflections. It's always been the reflections. Everything is a reflection. Think about every good story you've ever heard, every song that stayed in your memory. Are they really about the people in them, or are they showing us what's in ourselves? You'd be amazed what I could do with a single drop of water lying still on a leaf. Ah!" he said, ushering Willuna closer to the nearest mirror, "speaking of turning our insides out. I do believe I have something to show your friend the king." He stuck his nose right up to the glass. "Goodness me, he really is a handsome fellow, isn't he?"

They watched as a single figure of the undead parted from the mass of the enemy, shuffled its way to the foot of the drawbridge. Willuna frowned. She couldn't see the figure's face, but the cape, the armour, the sword, they were all achingly familiar. She knew this skeleton, but not by its bones.

And then she realized, the armour, the colours of the cape, they were the colours of the Family Wolf. She looked over to the young king standing stricken on the drawbridge, defenseless and pained. "Oh Anisim," she whispered.

***

"Father?" said Anisim.

***

Willuna rounded on the wizard. "You are a very bad man!"

"Did you all catch that?" The wizard turned, addressing his soldiers that were still in the room. "'A very bad man.'" There was no reaction. "Honestly," he said, completely disappointed, "It's like talking to-"

"Yes!"

Bodolomous spun back around and saw…

***

Idwal pulled on Anisim's arm again, harder this time. The Wolf soldiers were doing their best to protect their king, but the undead were so many that they were piled high enough in the moat to start climbing over the sides of the drawbridge. They had only moments to get inside the open gates before the courtyard would be overwhelmed.

And more still were pouring out of mirrors that the original arrivals had brought with them. Idwal glanced over and saw some dark room or cave through the glass, looking like it went on forever.

Sweat ran down his back. The smell of the undead pressed down on them like sewer water. Idwal's mouth tasted metallic, and he supposed this was what honest and true fear tasted like. He didn't know, because he had never in his life been this terrified before.

He tugged on the king's arm again, but he would have had as much luck trying to move one of the statue people at the Castle Owl. "Please, your Majesty, it's really time to go. Just a few steps backwards, that's a good king."

Anisim hadn't heard him. "Look at him," he said, staring as the remains of his father moaned and slumped their way towards him. "Even when he's dead he's far more the king than I."

Idwal looked over. "That's your father? He did that to your father? It's not like I loved the wizard before but this, this is despicable and wretched and…"

***

The wizard smiled as Idwal went on.

"…horrid and he's probably a eunuch."

The wizard's smile dropped.

***

Idwal had an idea. He wasn't at all sure it was what anyone would call a *good* idea. But being as it was the only one he had he thought he'd follow it through. He unlimbered his bow for the first time in the battle and zipped an arrow right into the late king's chest.

Anisim jolted. "You shot my father!" he said.

"Yes, terribly sorry. It's just that, well, I've of course heard a very great deal about the old boy and, um, from what I've heard, not that I'm saying I knew him personally at all of course, but if the stories were true about his temper then if a body did go and shoot and arrow into him your father-"

"Would have been angry." Anisim climbed out of his slouch and stood tall again. "Yes, he would have been *furious*. Whatever that thing is, it's no longer my father."

"Hooray!"

"If he was my father he'd have had your head off by now."

"Um, hooray?"

"He'd be kicking it around like a ball."

"Can we go inside now?"

"Oh," said Anisim, "absolutely. Back!" called the king. "Behind the walls!" And with Idwal at his side, he retreated into the courtyard, the portcullis slamming down behind them.

***

"As queen of the Family Owl I demand that you stop at once!"

"As the Evilest Magician Ever I say unto you 'nuts'."

"You'll fail," said Willuna. "You'll be defeated. And then you'll be mocked, and berated, and really made fun of and... and..."

"Yes?" said Bodolomous, leaning forward, hands clasped behind his back, enjoying himself thoroughly.

And that was it, wasn't it? Willuna took in the wizard's grin, and realized that he was looking forward to all that infamy. To all that chatter about him, even if it was to paint him as vile. All that attention...

"And then," said the princess, "we'll forget all about you."

The magician's face lost its amusement.

Willuna dug in. "You, magician, are nothing but a footnote-to-be."

"You said you wanted to hear my story," said the magician, his voice chilled. "You asked me why I'm doing all of this."

Willuna's triumph changed, turned sour. She had truly angered the wizard. She backed away a step, then two. "I've changed my-"

The magician's quick hand snaked out and grabbed her wrist. He dragged her along to the far wall of the room, up a set of winding stone stairs. "There's a single room," he said between his teeth, "a single room in all the kingdoms, a room made by infinite hands, hands that were in turn made by a man who was made by a girl, long ago." He brought her up onto a landing, brought her to the very edge to look out across the giant dark room, to take in how many more troops he still had to send. Hundreds. "Right now the contents of the room, the room made by the man made by the girl, those contents are rushing out to change everything."

And then Willuna knew. She knew who the magician was and who he had once been. She remembered a much younger magician, little more than a boy, who had made some name for himself with his amazing sleight-of-hand. She remembered him coming into her father's court and amazing all assembled. He had been fast, the very young man, and dazzling. All eyes had been glued fast to him, all ears tuned to the young magician's nervous patter. And that had been unacceptable to the very young princess who could never abide someone stealing her attention.

She remembered sneaking up behind the young magician and, as he had been launching into yet another illusion, finding in his stack of props and paraphernalia a rabbit, white with bright red eyes. The young magician had been a liar! He didn't know magic, he knew tricks. Tricks that were taking attention away from where it was supposed to be fixed, on her.

So she had set the rabbit free. And a dove. And a snake and a rat. They had jumped and flew and slithered and hopped off in every direction, unwinding the young magician's performance. The gasps and applause had turned to laughter. Willuna remembered that young magician dropping his head in humiliation and shame.

Her, this had all been about her. She had always wanted attention, and she had gotten it now in spades. And that attention had destroyed her world.

Bodolomous had seen the recognition in her eyes. He moved behind her and grabbed her shoulders, making sure she couldn't turn away from the scenes taking place in all those mirrors down below. "Right now," he said, "a farmer is tending his field, a miser is counting his coins, a mother is singing her child to sleep. None of them know that what they are doing right now will never matter again, not after this moment in time. All of them undone by what's coming out of the room created by the man created by the girl. I'm nothing? I'm nobody? I'm a foot-note to be? No, Queen Willuna of the Family Owl, I'm exactly what you made me."

"Please," said Willuna, tears dripping from her cheeks, "I was just a child."

From below something surged up, blocking their view. It was a man, a giant man, made of many dead men strung and sewed and roped together, heaving and moving as one. It was powerful and terrifying.

It lunged through a mirror big as a house, ducking as it made its way through, heading out to crush the defenders of the Castle Wolf.

***

The portcullis twisted, screeched like a banshee as the undead giant plucked it out of the wall. Skeleton soldiers oozed through the opening, bone feet clicking against the stone of the courtyard. The defenders pressed back and back again.

Idwal aimed and fired, aimed and fired. Arrows weren't much use against the rank and file of the enemy, the arrowheads clattering uselessly in rib cages and empty eye sockets. But the giant was held together by straps, moved by pulleys, and Idwal found those to be fine targets. He fired again and a sling of leather snapped free of the beast. A hand disintegrated, the individual fingers tumbling down to the ground. Some smashed apart, others clambered up and joined the mob of their undead brothers and sisters.

But then he was out of arrows. He scrambled around, looking for more. He knew the archers on the walls above had extras, but the stairs were cut off. There had to be more somewhere on this level though, what kind of self-respecting war-oriented castle didn't have surplus pointy things lying about?

And then someone did something rather naughty with the sun. The space all around Idwal went dark. He looked up. The giant's foot was sailing down at him, the individual cadavers that made up the foot reaching down for him, mouths open and groaning. Well, thought Idwal, that's that then.

Anisim charged into him, picking the farmer up, knocking the wind out of him, tumbling them both to the ground to roll out of the way. The giant foot touched down beside them, surprisingly quiet, it didn't seem quite proper for a giant foot to hit the ground without some kind of bone-shaking boom. Half-fleshed heads turned to look at them from inside the collective shape of the foot. As the giant leg lifted, pulleys and straps creaking and groaning, the skeletons making up the sole of the foot had Idwal's magic bow in their hands. They snapped it, bit at the string, broke it again and again into smaller and smaller pieces.

Idwal watched it go with regret. One of the mere two things that made him special in this world had just been destroyed. He was that much closer to being plain and normal again, and he found that he didn't like the thought of that at all.

King Anisim had no trouble at all finding a new quiver of arrows and a spare bow to go with them. In fact they were both just lying on the top of a closer barrel no more than three steps away, which Idwal figured was just the kind of luck he was having these days. Anisim held them out to Idwal.

"I can't," Idwal shouted over the clamour. "I'm no archer. My bow was magic."

"That magic had to draw from somewhere!" Anisim shouted back. He pointed up at the giant. There, in the mass of rotting waving arms and legs was a great knot of leather, the size of a child. All of the other ropes and pulleys and straps radiated out in sloppy, uneven waves like the work of a drunken spider. "Do you see it?" cried the king. "That's for you! That target is the reason for the turnip, the reason why you met the magician, all of the things that have happened to you to bring you to this very moment to shoot that one knot! The bow wasn't magic farmer, the magic was you!"

"Me?"

"Trust me!"

Idwal accepted the bow. He pulled an arrow from the quiver. It just seemed like the right arrow for the occasion. He notched the arrow to the string, took aim. The giant's knot looked big as a boulder, as easy to hit as air. He could do this. He aimed. He told himself to just let the rest of the world fade away. There was just the arrow and bow, which were extensions of him, and in his mind the knot was already split, the giant's demise a done deed. He fired.

Sort of.

The arrow dribbled over his fist to stick in the ground by his foot.

The king scratched his head. He shrugged. "Or maybe it was the bow."

"It was completely the bow."

And then, as if things weren't really just absolutely rotten enough, the ground in the middle of the courtyard began to cave in.

***

Willuna saw it all through the mirrors. Saw the Wolf soldiers pressed back toward the castle's last refuge, the keep. Saw Anisim staggering, growing tired from the fight. Saw the farmer's really awful effort with the bow and arrow. They were all going to die, all because of her.

So she turned to the wizard and said, "I will marry you."

CHAPTER 20

The magician turned. Looked at her. Emotions chased each other around his face, disbelief and glee and amazement vying for control of his eyes and mouth. "What?" he said, like there was no possibility at all that he might have heard her correctly.

Her heart drowning inside of her, Willuna carried on. "I will marry you, join with you. "I will become your better half, I will be your wife. You wanted attention? Well here it is, all you want and more, waiting for you on the other end of a simple 'I do.' Now call off your army."

"After."

"But they'll be dead!"

The wizard didn't hear her. He clapped his hands. The hairless, and quite often fleshless, skulls below turned up to look at the pair of them on the stone landing high above. "Hi, everyone?" said the wizard, suddenly chipper. "Hi there, hi hi. Um, yes, right, before you toddle off to maim and kill and destroy et cetera, I was just wondering if any of you might have been a priest before, you know, well... Now I of course realize that you all have rotten jelly for brains but if you could just bare down for the tiniest of moments and give it a really good think."

There was silence down below as the cadavers worked this request through as best they could. Finally a hand raised up in the middle of the mob.

"Oh, yes? You were?" The wizard leaned forward. The hand, missing three fingers, see-sawed in the air. "Most of you was a priest? Good enough. Wonderful! If you could join us up here, thanks ever so much. The rest of you make way, make way!" As the undead mostly-priest made his slow way up the stone stairs the wizard turned to Willuna. "And I thought I was excited about destroying everything everyone holds dear." He gave a childish clap of his hands. "Hooray!"

***

The blacksmiths picked up hammers, the stable-boys found pitchforks. Cooks came from the kitchens, stewards brought out polished knives and forks. Everyone in the castle joined together now for this last moment before the Wolf Kingdom died, withered, and was blown away.

The rotting army poured through the gates, over each other, through each other, like mud through a child's fingers.

The ground behind them continued to crumble, caving in.

"Go down swinging," said the king.

"Will cowering do me any good?" said Idwal.

"I'm afraid not."

"Then swinging it is." Just then, Willuna's dreams of being in songs and stories whispered through Idwal's memories. He wondered if he would be remembered at all. Probably not. Even though he was fighting beside his friend who was a king, he himself was just a country boy after all, and nothing very exciting rhymed with "farmer".

He wondered if dying would hurt very much.

Anisim raised his great sword into the air. One final rally. "Let them come, sons and daughters of the wolf! Let them know the price of your castle and kingdom!"

They charged, so few against so many, like pebbles thrown against whitecap waves. Everything was motion and noise around Idwal. He was sure every flash or flicker he saw was the deathblow meant for him.

A pick-axe whirled past Idwal's shoulder. It smashed into a skeleton so hard that the undead soldier flew apart, arms and legs and rib-bones twirling white and yellow every which way. And then there were more missiles - sledge-hammers, kerosene lanterns, chisels and logging axes and shovels.

Idwal spun around.

The dwarves had come. First came the familiar seven, climbing up out of the hole in the courtyard, blinking like moles in the sunlight. Dirty and beautiful. Then more sprung up, bellowing, broad shoulders flexing, thick fingers clinging the handles of their tools.

Cosimo laughed at Idwal's stunned expression. "Did you think there were only seven of us?"

***

"Oh. Um, right. Well I promise to try and be a good husband and not kill too many people unless they really deserve it which, you must admit, quite a few do."

They were away from the great room, down halls, behind doors, the battle noises drowned by floors and walls of black stone. They were in some dank room, indistinguishable from any number of other dank rooms they had passed on their way here.

Willuna and the wizard stood side-by-side, her slim cool hand held lightly in his clammy paw. Before them the once mostly-priest mumbled and groaned some incomprehensible syllables, then turned to her.

The vow came easy to her. The words had been with her since she'd been a little girl. She said them quietly, her eyes cast down. "Before now, I was nothing but the sweet anticipation of this day. Time begins only now, at this moment, as I join myself with you."

Beside her, the magician wiped a tear from his eye. Was this an opening? Was there still some humanity left inside him?

Willuna raised her head and peered around. "Does this seem quite right to you?"

"What do you mean? It's right in the sense of evil triumphing over good."

"What I mean is, here we are, a queen and the Most Evil Man Alive getting married and, well…" She waved a hand around the empty room. "Don't you think such an occasion should be a bit more…"

"Grand?"

"Exactly! There should be a great hall."

"I've got one right upstairs."

"And people celebrating."

"I can make my minions clap. Calling out our praises might be a bit of a problem."

Willuna turned to the wizard. "Can we postpone? Just a slight delay while we make more suitable arrangements."

"Well…" He wagged a finger at her. "I'm not stopping my conquest for this."

"Conquest? Oh, that." Willuna waved a dismissive hand at the thought of the war going on below. "I'm surprised such an immense undertaking doesn't require more supervision from its evil mastermind."

"I admit I'm quite close to chewing my fingernails."

"Go on then. I'll arrange, you pillage. We'll meet up later for drinks. Oh, before you go, have you given any thought to a colour scheme?"

The magician scratched his head. "Orange and blue?"

"You *are* evil."

The magician started for the doorway. Willuna held up a finger. "Oh, just one more thing," she said. "I'll need a helper or two."

***

The giant unwound. Severed straps curled in the air, snapped like whips. The undead members of its body tumbled apart, pattering to the ground, cracking. Bits and pieces skittered across the courtyard to be smashed by hammers and skewered by swords.

A battle. A genuine bit of warfare, and he had survived. Idwal was bruised, his arms sore from all that sword-swinging and archery. Clammy sweat clung to him like a second skin. But the lightning-sick smell of fear was leaving him, slicked off him by the breeze that made its gentle way through the courtyard.

Soon there was only one undead figure left on this side of the mirrors and moat. It still shambled forward, coming to join the battle, dressed in its regal black and grey.

Idwal saw Anisim start forward. He caught up with the king but Anisim waved him off.

"It's okay," said Anisim. He stood at the entrance to the courtyard, under the archway, waiting for what remained of his father to come close. "You know farmer, I never got a hug from him. Not even a handshake. You know what I wanted most of all? Just peace. Just a quiet moment that was all my own. Well," he said, tightening his grip on the handle of his sword, "I now give it to him."

With that, Anisim raised his sword to the level of his dead father's neck and gave it a mighty swing.

***

Bodolomous stood on his stone landing above the great mirror room, watching as Wolf soldiers approached the other side of his magic mirrors to smash them to bits, leaving them black and empty on this side.

The farmer was there too, pressing a hand against the glass of one of the mirrors, trying to get through. "I quite dislike him," said the wizard. "Right then," he called out, his voice echoing around the room, "send more troops through. Let's get this done, I've got a marriage to get to."

Nothing happened. Bodolomous took a step closer to the edge and looked down. There were no more of his minions below him. He held up a hand, palm turned up, and muttered a bit of magical this and that. A fireball blossomed above his hand, the flames turning over on themselves. He threw the fireball left, illuminating the room's far corners. No troops. He whipped up another fireball and cast it right. Nothing.

This wasn't right. He should still have hundreds of minions left. He'd had minions making minions making minions. He hadn't expected a bunch of undead folk to be fantastic warriors, what with the atrophied muscles and goo for brains. He had been depending on numbers. Great big numbers. Numbers with enough digits that it would get tiring trying to write them down.

Where had his army gone?

***

'Is there no hope for her then?"

Idwal and the king stood on the battlements, looking out over the flat fields before the castle. Wolf soldiers were moving about in small units, breaking the last of the mirrors and poking at bits and pieces of the undead to make sure they weren't up to causing any more trouble.

"We don't know that the magician has her," said the king. "I say there's always hope. The fact that *I'm* the one saying that is reason for hope in and of itself. And, well, I hacked off my father's head today. I mean honestly, who could have seen that coming?"

A round of grunted cursing made them look down into the courtyard below. A familiar crystal casket was being shoved out of the opening in the ground. It thumped down, choice bits of its occupant jiggling in a most appealing fashion.

Anisim led the way down through the dwarves. He knelt beside the casket. "She's breath-taking," he said. "Who is she?"

Idwal put a comforting hand on the shoulder of the nearest miserable dwarf. "This is Snow-Drop," Idwal said. "She was poisoned by her evil step-mother. Who, word has it, was a queen of someplace. And also a witch."

"A queen?" Anisim looked up. "Really? Murderous villain! I'll have words with her."

"Please good sir," said Cosimo, wringing his cap in his hands, "your farmer friend here, he told us your kiss was magic."

Everyone in the courtyard turned to look at Idwal. He waved his hands. "That's just what I *heard*, I swear!"

***

Bodolomous hustled through his great dark castle, feet kicking the hem of his robe out in front of him, calling out for Rotter and the rest of his minions. He really shouldn't have made the castle so big and dark, it was just impossible to find anything.

Having searched the rest of the halls, the courtyard, the towers and the dungeons, Bodolomous finally made his way to the great hall where his wedding to Princess Willuna was to take place. At least he had that much to look forward to. Head down, wondering if there was some grim dark corner of the castle he had missed, he walked up to the young queen-to-be. He was feeling a bit sheepish. He was going to have to ask her for her helpers back so they could help search for the rest of his missing army. It wouldn't look very powerful or evil, losing platoons of smelly cadaverous soldiers.

"Ah, princess," he said, "a word if I might."

The princess gave him a smile. "Isn't it wonderful?" She waved her hands around the room.

The wizard supposed she had put up some decorations or flowers or something, but he was feeling a bit too embarrassed to look anywhere but at his feet. "Yes yes," he said, "never seen the like. The thing is," he toed the ground, "I'm trying to conduct a slaughter in the next room over."

"Oh, right! How's that going? Look, we made bunting!"

"If you must know, the whole laying low of mine enemies has hit a bit of a snag."

"I really should have my father give me away. It's too bad we ran afoul of that old woman."

Bodolomous looked up. "Old woman?"

"That stoning spell she used must be the wickedest bit of magic ever!"

"That?" Bodolomous sniffed. "Wicked? Ha!" He pulled a stoppered bottle from the sleeve of his robe, gave its faintly glowing contents a bit of a swirl. "I figured that one out in a night!"

"Impressive," said the princess, nodding. "Although to be honest it's very easy to just copy someone else's-"

Bodolomous whipped out a second bottle. "Copy? Me? Ha and ha again!" He shook the second bottle. "Done and undone in the very same night. What do you think of that?"

"That's an antidote?"

"Of course."

"Astounding!"

"You're too kind." Bodolomous smiled and rocked a bit on his feet. He was genuinely getting to like this girl. Seemed like she knew real evil when she saw it. "Now, about my war. It would appear I've run a bit short of..." Looking up, he got his first really good look around the room. His good feelings towards the girl instantly vanished. "You made furniture out of them!" He thrust his finger out.

His army was here. All of them. They been positioned to form rows and rows of pews, some sitting on the backs of others. And where they'd run out of space for pews, they'd started to fill in the seating spaces as an audience.

The princess gave him a sickly grin. "Too much?" she said.

CHAPTER 21

Tears dropped from bulbous dwarven noses. The crystal casket lid was raised up, followed by a milk-pale hand. Lips quivering, noses sniffling, the dwarves watched as Anisim drew Snow-Drop to her perfect little feet.

She looked up at him with her great dark eyes. "You're not a dwarf," she said. "I can tell."

Watching the dwarves watching Snow-Drop watching Anisim, something suddenly occurred to Idwal. "Sorry," he said, "but your step-mum, she was a bit of a witch, wasn't she? Did she happen to know anything about reflections?"

***

The great dark hall echoed with the wizard's bellows. "It's high time you gave me just a smidgeon of respect!" He turned from Willuna and yelled at the furniture/undead. "Get up you idiots! Go and kill something!" They blinked at him, not moving from their places. The wizard whirled back to Willuna. "What did you do to my wonderful hordes? Make them move!"

Willuna jutted her chin up into the air. "I'll thank you not to take that tone with me. I am, after all-"

The wizard howled with rage and clamped a great clammy hand around her wrist. He dragged her behind him, bruising her, pulling her back into the mirror room.

The magician pulled her to a halt right at the edge of the landing. "Send them through!" he bellowed into her face.

"I don't have enough words to tell you just how much I refuse."

"I could kill you!"

"I'm not afraid."

"I could torture you."

"I stand ready."

And stand she did, poised and regal. She really did feel unafraid then, like nothing he could do would ever touch her again. But then he reached into the sleeve of his robe and pulled out the antidote, the potion that could save her father. The wizard dangled it over the edge of the landing.

"Send them through, or I promise you your father will remain a bird-stand forever." He shook the bottle.

"Don't!"

"Send them through!"

"Please!"

"Alas," said the magician, and drew back his arm to hurl the bottle.

"Hold!"

Willuna looked down and laid eyes on the most wonderful sight she'd ever seen. Seven dwarves, Anisim, and Idwal were piling through one of the mirrors below. Oh, and that twit from the glass casket too, all cleavage-y and glassy-eyed.

"What are you all doing here?" said the magician, sounding really rather put out.

"Your mentor had a step-daughter," said Anisim.

"I told you I could find him!" said Snow-Drop.

Willuna stepped back as the wizard squinted, peering down from the edge at the girl below. "You, I remember you. Boy, you certainly grew up."

"Uh-huh," said Snow-Drop, "mostly my boobs."

"Give up magician!" called up the king.

"But I really want to win!" The wizard thrust out an arm. From the hallway behind came his jesters, his last loyal few, bounding and jumping and leaping from the giddy heights of the landing down to the floor below. He grabbed Willuna around her waist and hauled her away, back to the great hall.

He scrambled to a stop, manhandling the wildcat in his arms. "Right, listen you all!" He addressed himself to the putrid pews. "The wedding's off. So you can all toddle off and return to your hacking and your maiming."

"Don't listen to him!" said Willuna from back over his shoulder.

"I made you!" The wizard wagged a warning finger at them. "Each and every one!"

"Yes! That's right! He pulled you from your sleep, wrenched you from your peace and quiet!"

"Well, okay, yes, I suppose. Is that what this little mutiny is all about? Fine." The wizard smiled his bestest smile at the undead. "You lot hustle on down to the mirror room, kill the intruders, and voila, you're back in your graves by sundown. Deal?"

"Oh sure, that was convincing. And after the mirror room it will be 'Oh, could you just pillage this one last tiny little kingdom for me?'"

The wizard shuffled around, trying to stare the princess in the face, which is not the easiest thing to do when said person is flung over your shoulder. "Will you keep quiet?!"

"And then after that it will be, 'Oh, dreadfully sorry, forgot about this castle that needs a really good sieging, completely slipped my-'"

The wizard plunked her down on her feet and clapped a hand over her mouth. Willuna bit it. "It will never end!" she said.

The wizard made an odd little gesture. A strip from the hem of Willuna's dress ripped itself off and wrapped itself around her head, gagging her. Willuna twisted the magician's ear. Another gesture, and another strip snaked up to tie her hands behind her back.

"Now hear this! I pledge to every and all undead here today…" He looked over and caught sight of just how much higher the hem of Willuna's dress was. "My goodness," he said, "that's a lot of leg. Ankles are kind of skinny but-"

Willuna stomped her foot in fury, her face turning a ferocious shade of red under the gag. The wizard shook off his admiration and turned back to the cadavers. "Right," he said. "So, about that eternal peace."

***

The jesters were done, cut apart and twitching on the floor. Idwal and his friends were free to climb the long line of stone stairs up to the landing. To find Willuna and free her. But then the landing above was full of the undead, piling up, pouring over the edge, falling and cracking apart at their feet. Some of them appeared to be decorated with bunting.

The wizard was up there amongst them, holding Willuna at his side. "The princess has come to weep," he said. "I have come to gloat. And you have come to die."

There were too many, just too many. They continued to pour over, a deluge, a flood. The enemy circled around, so many of them that their numbers were lost to the darkness in one direction, silhouetted from a distant window in the other. Now even the mirrors were cut off. They were ten, the enemy hundreds.

Idwal looked up to the landing, saw the princess looking back down, terror in her great round eyes. He of course understood now what it meant to be a hero. He'd hung around Anisim long enough. It wasn't skill with a sword, it wasn't presence on a battlefield. "Hero" and "sacrifice" were the very same word. He wondered if maybe people would sing about him in times to come.

He pulled his fiddle from its string around his neck. He placed his bow to the strings. And he played. The tune jumped and jigged around the great hall, wiggling its way into the undead's ears. They danced. They sprang. They shimmied and spun and kicked up (and occasionally *off*) their feet. Their thousands of stomping feet added a thundering bass-line to the fiddle's high tune.

Above them, the magician raved. He flung another strip from the hem of Willuna's dress to bound the farmer's hands, but the princess gave him a shove, tumbling him back into the hallway behind them to fall on the stone floor. The strip of cloth fluttered down past the farmer's face.

Idwal led the undead army to the large window at the far end of the room… and then out. The undead followed, tumbling out the window to fall and smash themselves to pieces on the crags and spires of the mountain-sides below.

And then there was silence.

CHAPTER 22

Gone, the farmer was gone. Willuna stood blinking at the far window, dumb to the world around her.

The wizard stumbled past her to look down over the edge. Gone, they were all gone, all of his wonderful army, his chance to make his name. A last few leg bones twitched and clicked against the stone floor below, and that was it.

"I won't have it!" he screamed. He rounded on Willuna. "You! You will still surrender to me, you and the king and your stumpy little friends! Don't move!" he shouted at Anisim and the dwarves below. He whipped out the bottle of antidote and tore out the stopper. He held it over the edge again, tipping it. The liquid inside kissed the bottle's mouth's rim. "How many, eh? How many will pass through your courtyard, cursing your name? How many will see all those people you couldn't save? Say you surrender!"

Willuna struggled, wanting to scream back.

"How much is enough?" the wizard continued. He let the potion drip drip drip out to the floor below. "Who could this have saved? A butcher? And this? A stable-hand? Maybe a cook? Tell me! Tell me you yield! Call me your master!"

He flicked his fingers. The cloth unknotted itself from around Willuna's head and drooped down to the ground. He leaned in close to her, turned his ear to her lips. "Let me hear the words."

Willuna leaned forward and spoke quietly right into his ear. "You..."

"Yes?"

"...are..."

"Yes? Say it!"

"...leaking."

A dark damp spot was spreading on the sleeve of his robes. He reached in and pulled out the flask that contained his version of the stoning potion. It was just a sliver of a crack, looking like a tiny white line of lightning in the glass. It had broken when Willuna knocked him down into the hall. Potion oozed out.

The wizard's hand crackled and trembled, and then turned to stone. Willuna could trace the transformation up his arm, across his chest, the noise much like the crackling of a fire but somehow much drier.

The wizard's eyes were wild. He remembered the antidote in his other hand. He brought it towards himself, trying to upend it on himself, fighting the stone that laced through his body.

Willuna lunged forward, drove her shoulder into his arm. The bottle flew out. Before the wizard could shout, his mouth was stone.

The antidote spun out, away, the liquid spinning around in the belled bottom of the bottle. "Catch it!" she screamed.

There was a scramble on the floor below, dwarves jostling a king as they all reached up. The king's fingertips touched the bottle, sent it tumbling. It bobbled and tumbled down and across sixty-nine stumpy fingers and thumbs (Egon had lost his right pinky in a slightly terrible pick-axe incident many years ago). And then there were no more hands, only stone floor.

Snow-Drop dove to the ground and the bottle finally came to a spectacularly well-cushioned stop on her chest. She grasped the bottle with both hands and smiled up. "Did I win?" she said.

Above them on the landing Willuna sighed in relief. Her eyes then turned to the window at the end of the room, and she began to cry.

***

There was a breeze nagging at him, persistent and cold. His arms squirmed around, looking for a blanket that wasn't there. That would teach him to leave the windows open overnight. Someone grabbed him by the collar and gave him a good shaking. He supposed it was his father trying to get him up, fields don't plow themselves, don't you know? He wanted to be a good boy, but couldn't quite shake himself awake.

His eyes flickered open, and he had the rather unpleasant impression that he was dangling from an incredible height over some very pointy dark rocks that thrust up from the ground far below. He let his eyes drift closed again, he must still be dreaming, he couldn't recall ever having some kind of dark and ominous mountain range in his bedroom.

The breeze cut off. His bed seemed to grow hard and uncomfortable beneath him. Voices bobbed and dipped around him like flowers sailing downstream.

"...breathing at least..."

"...bump on his head..."

"...had an army come crashing down on his noodle, bound to shake loose some brains..."

He left his parents behind and swam up back into his body, surfacing behind his eyes. They were arranged around him - the king, the girl from the crystal casket, the seven smiling dwarves, and the princess. He sat up and his brain did somersaults inside his skull.

"I'm alive?" he said.

"And a hero," said the king.

"You were hanging on a pointy bit out on the wall," said one of the dwarves.

"I think I lost my fiddle."

"Don't worry about it," said Anisim, extending a hand. "We'll get you a new one."

Anisim hoisted him to his feet. "Come," said the king, "let's make sure the magician can never find his way back to us again."

"The magician!" Idwal looked around as the others moved off to smash the mirrors, leaving him alone with Willuna.

"Don't worry," said the princess, pointing up to the newly-made statue on the ledge.

They stood there, not looking at each other. The royal and the peasant.

"So," he said.

"So," she said back.

"I guess we should…" Idwal waved at the others.

"Help with the mirrors, yes."

And so, after another moment of them both wanting to say everything but managing to say absolutely nothing, they separated and joined the others.

***

The antidote worked. They tested it on the magician, bringing him back to life. Willuna had been tempted to leave him a statue, gazing out that one window forever, but she couldn't find that kind of cruelty in herself. Leaving the newly restored wizard under the guard of the dwarves, she joined Anisim who was finishing up with one of the last few mirrors.

He gave her a proper, handsome bow and handed over a pick-axe. "My lady," he said, "if you would be so good."

She curtsied in a most proper and pretty manner back, then took the tool and, with a mighty bellow, smashed down the mirror before them. They watched as it wobbled, the glass raining down, and then fell over on its back.

"Fun!"

Anisim smiled. "You're a vision when you're breaking things."

"I think I've found my calling. And you, good sir, maybe you'll get to hang up your sword for just a little while. I heard you cut off you father's head by the way, how did that go?"

"Go? It went off and to the left."

"Very funny. I seem to recall you saying you'd like to make something rather than merely destroying. Do you have any ideas?"

"Painting is out, that's for sure." He turned and looked back over his shoulder. Snow-Drop was at one of the other mirrors, waving a sledgehammer. She was of course holding the wrong end, knocking the handle against the glass. "I thought I might make some babies." He turned to her. "I can't explain it, but-"

"She's lovely. Ankles are a bit thick if you ask me, but... A peasant? What will people think?"

Anisim thought for a moment, his ruggedly handsome brow frowning down. "You know," he said, "I think they'll think it's love."

"And what about me?" said Willuna. "You and I, we were always supposed to be together."

"Is that what you really want?" asked Anisim. He grinned at her and nodded over at the farmer.

"Him? He's not... I mean, he can't really... He's just... Stop grinning at me!" Willuna stomped her little foot. "Go away and make your babies!"

"I think I just might. But first, there's apparently a very evil witch running loose in the world that I would like to have some words with." Smiling at her, Anisim bowed his way away. He turned and walked over to Snow-Drop.

Willuna watched Snow-Drop point up at the mirror she was trying to destroy. She pointed a beautiful finger up at the glass. "That's a really big mirror," she said in that breathless way of talking she had.

"Stupid, *stupid* babies," Willuna muttered to herself.

Only one mirror remained. The others gathered around it, passed through. Willuna stood before it, waiting for the farmer to approach. "Oh farmer," she said.

"Yeah?"

"'Yeah?' That's an awfully informal way to address your queen."

"You're not queen yet." Idwal waggled the bottle of antidote.

The magician was coming down the stairs from the landing, dragging his right foot behind him. He'd stayed up out of sight for the most part, worried that a peep out of him might cancel out the princess' mercy. But now he was hellowing, waving an arm as he made his slow way down all those stone steps. "Well!" he called out. "It has been a day, hasn't it? Lessons learned, faux pas forgiven, errors erased? It's just, my foot you see." He raised the hem of his robe to show that he hadn't received quite enough of the antidote, that one foot still remained as stone.

Willuna ignored him. She saw only the farmer before him with his simple clothes and his ever-sheepish expression. She tilted her head one way, the other, appraising him, watched him blush under the scrutiny.

She pointed at the magician. "You," she commanded, "close your eyes."

"Right you are," replied the wizard, "only too glad to help."

She pointed at the farmer. "You," she requested, "close your eyes too."

He did, without question, trusting her completely. Before she could convince herself otherwise she rushed forward and kissed him, quick, a hummingbird's peck.

His eyes snapped open. "But... but... but I'm just a-"

"Yes."

"And you're a-"

"That's right. And a princess expects that when she kisses someone, he kiss her right back."

And so he did.

Then, hand in hand, they passed through the last mirror, back to the land of the Wolves. And as they went through, their free hands brushed the wood frame of the mirror. It teetered, it tottered, and before the wizard even knew they were gone, it keeled over and fell against the floor.

AFTER

So that was that. The last mirror was gone. There was water around the great dark castle, but it was full of goo and slime and not nearly clean enough to ever cast a proper reflection.

Bodolomous sat for some time on the stone steps, chin on his fist, contemplating all that he had done. He'd been powerful. He'd been rotten. He'd kidnapped royalty. He'd been the Most Evil Man Alive. And despite all that effort and all that deviousness, here he was, all alone again.

He wondered if there were enough bits lying around to construct a new minion. Seemed like a lot of effort though, especially when minions couldn't talk. They couldn't ever say nice things to him, compliment him when he was having a good hair day.

"Huh," he said. Because he now realized that that was what he had been after all along. A friend. A companion. Someone who would shut their eyes because you requested it, not because you commanded it.

He supposed the princess had found this truth too. Hadn't she also done the wrong thing, trying to transform herself outwardly in order to ensnare a man? She had done the right thing eventually, giving of herself, becoming the person who would one day be a very good queen, no matter what man she married.

The farmer seemed to have learned the same lesson. It seemed that the farmer had worked so hard at pretending to be what he was not, going so far as to set up a marriage with a woman he wasn't truly in love with because she would help complete his disguise. But the hick had managed to change; he'd stopped avoiding the world because he thought he was supposed to; he'd fought when he'd had something worth fighting for, and had gained a princess for his troubles. Not a bad day's work, that.

"Huh," he said again. It wasn't profound by any means, but it summed things up nicely. Like the others, Bodolomous the wizard had taken a long, circuitous route to find this one thing out:

That maybe, in the end, there was no such thing as a shortcut to love.

ABOUT THE AUTHOR

Daniel Fox was once kicked in the shin by Fox Mulder's little sister.

Made in the USA
Lexington, KY
27 January 2012